HAPPY TOWN

MUST BE DESTROYED

JAMES HARRIS

Illustrations by Jennifer Naalchigar

HODDER

HODDER CHILDREN'S BOOKS

First published in Great Britain in 2022 by Hodder & Stoughton

1 3 5 7 9 10 8 6 4 2

Text copyright © James Harris, 2022
Illustrations copyright © Jennifer Naalchigar, 2022

The moral rights of the author and illustrator have been asserted.

A CIP catalogue record for this book
is available from the British Library.

ISBN 978 1 444 95970 3

Typeset in Museo Slab by Avon DataSet Ltd, Alcester, Warwickshire
Printed and bound in Great Britain by Clays Ltd. Elcograf S.p.A.

The paper and board used in this book
are made from wood from responsible sources.

Hodder Children's Books
An imprint of Hachette Children's Group
Part of Hodder & Stoughton Ltd
Carmelite House
50 Victoria Embankment
London EC4Y 0DZ

An Hachette UK Company
www.hachette.co.uk
www.hachettechildrens.co.uk

To my sunny, funny D.
Keep dancing! Yay! x

Chapter 1

HELLO SUNSHINE

'Cookie dough, caramel and cabbage,' said Ishy.

'Shut up, Ishy,' I said.

'OK. Coffee, cod and carrot,' said Ishy.

'Shush! What's the blue one again?' I said.

'It's still bubblegum,' said the ice-cream man. 'Like it was when I told you five minutes ago.'

I had been standing at the hatch of the Daddy Cool ice-cream van trying to decide which three flavours of ice cream to have for around ten minutes. Ishy was being helpful by listing various combinations for me, and the ice-cream man was being helpful by not shouting at me to hurry up and choose because there was a queue behind me, even though his eyes were clearly telling me that I should hurry up and choose because there was a queue behind me.

In fairness to me, there were twenty flavours of ice cream listed on the board, and if I was picking three of them to go on my wifflewaffle sugar cone, then that would mean there were potentially, ooh, let me work it out ... *20 times 3 times the square root of* ...

There were potentially a gazillion different combinations.

Yes, I am good at maths. Thank you for noticing.

I was pretty sure I wanted pistachio, but would that go better with salted caramel or honeycomb crunch? And then what would be the topper? Bubblegum? I thought not but then again maybe?

I sighed and turned to the next person in the queue. It was Charlotte Actually, a girl from my year. Charlotte was tall, and blonde, and strong, with piercing eyes and an easy smile. Wherever she was, and whatever she was doing, she always looked *right*, like she was the perfect person to be *there*, doing *that*.

'You go,' I said. 'I need some time to . . .'

'Triple chocolate on plain cornet, with sprinkles, nutty crumble, no sauce, thank you,' said Charlotte to the ice-cream man. 'And could you do it quickly, please; my dance class starts in ten minutes. Thank you.'

Charlotte was a girl who knew what she wanted. She was the perfect ice-cream customer. But how could she be so sure?

There are a gazillion combinations, Charlotte, I said to myself, *and all but one of them are not the best combination.*

Perhaps she was not as good at maths as I am.

I mooched away from the ice-cream van and sat on a nearby moss-covered wall. Ishy bounded up, licking the remnants of his second ice cream of the day from around his mouth.

'Cookie dough, cauliflower and chorizo,' he said.

'You're not helping,' I said.

'Judging by the queue, you've got ten minutes to decide before the van goes. Do you reckon I can hop along the length of this wall, backwards?' he added, because he is a total goof.

As Ishy teetered and tottered on the wall, I watched the people of Owt queueing for ice cream in the bright, golden sunshine of a summer's early evening. None of them looked worried or confused, they just looked as though knowing exactly what ice cream you want is the easiest thing in the world. I shook my head and said 'weird' because they *are* weird and then I pushed my two-pronged infrared schnozzdongle up my nose.

'Yow!' said Ishy, falling from the wall and executing the opposite of a perfect dismount on the pavement. 'Ta-daaa! And now we know I can't hop backwards along this wall. I see you are zapping your allergies with nonsense again.'

6

'Sdop gallig id donzenz,' I said.

'I will stop calling it nonsense when it stops being nonsense.' He cracked open a can of Bubblejooce with a click-𝕱𝕺𝕺𝕺𝕺𝕾𝕳, fizzy fuel for his irritating banter. 'Aaaaah yeah! The fourth can of the day is always the best, just like the first three and the ones that come afterwards.'

My two-pronged infrared schnozzdongle is a battery pack connected to two light-up plastic nodules, one nodule for each nostril. I push the nodules into my nose and they zap the pollen and other allergens that get up there with infrared light, thus a) stopping me from sneezing, yay! and b) making my nose glow red like a traffic light, no yay! I sneeze a lot this time of year, and I am lucky enough to be called Leeza, which should tell you exactly how lucky I am generally. This is one reason why I don't like making choices – luck is against me.

'Ow, Leeza Sneezer,' said G-Dog. 'How's it glowing? Harhaaar!'

Oh, but of course G-Dog was around at this

precise moment! More excellent luck!

G-Dog was in our class at school. He was almost as wide as he was tall, and muscular in a way that made him look like fifteen potatoes in a bag made for five. He was a big, clumsy pain in the bum who thought he was funny but absolutely wasn't. He was squatting by the exhaust pipe of a nearby parked car, stuffing a banana in there. It looked a bit like he was feeding the car, but if cars did need feeding G-Dog was exactly the kind of boy who wouldn't. Basically whatever he was doing, he was definitely hoping it would annoy somebody because G-Dog really worked hard at being annoying.

'Whad id he doig wid dose badadas?' I asked Ishy as we watched G-Dog move towards another parked car.

'Dunnooooo,' Ishy burped. 'Did you hear that? I burped a whole word. Where's my trophy?' He chugged the last of his Bubblejooce. 'Hey, do you reckon if I spin around twenty times I could walk in a straight line to the ice-cream van, and do you reckon if I did that you'd be ready to choose an ice cream?'

I pulled my schnozzdongle out of my nose.

PLOP.

Yes, it went 'plop'. It goes 'plop' when I pull it out, because having to stick a glowing two-pronged plastic thing into the front of my face isn't undignified enough, because I am lucky that way. But at least I knew I wouldn't sneeze for twenty minutes or so.

And maybe I *was* ready to choose an ice cream. I was pretty sure pistachio was the way to go, although now I thought about it, chocolate would also work as a base layer, with maybe strawberry in the middle?

I could see the last person in the queue getting served at the van's hatch so I picked up the pace a little, arriving just as the customer was handed a vanilla 99.

Vanilla . . . I always forgot about vanilla . . .

'You again. Any chance I can sell you an ice

cream this time?' said the ice-cream man with a smile.

'Yes!' I said. 'I would like . . . um . . .'

Approximately a gazillion combinations of ice cream danced and twirled in my imagination.

'I'll have . . .'

'Good grief!' said the ice-cream man.

'I'll choose, I will!' I said.

'Duck!' he said, pointing out of his hatch at the sky behind me.

'Duck?' I said. 'Is that a new flavour or—'

'GET DOWN!' he hollered.

I turned and lifted my eyes, peering high into the sky to see what looked like . . . OK, it was moving pretty fast but it looked like a wobbly lime-green blob of jelly, flickering with pale-green flames, streaking across the evening sky towards us. It was trailing a flume of purple smoke behind it.

'Did someone order jelly with their ice cream?' said Ishy.

In the time it took for him to say it, the fiery

blob had halved the distance between us. It was moving like a rocket made of jam.

'What do we . . . I mean, which way should I . . . ?'

'Shift, Leeza!' said Ishy.

It was heading straight for me but I was rooted to the spot. I didn't know whether to leap to the left or leap to the right. Left would be a softer landing with the grass verge, but right would mean I could hide behind a bin.

I heard the ice-cream man mutter, 'So it begins once more', which was odd, but then I forgot all about it as Ishy launched himself at my middle, taking both of us to the ground as the superfast gumball hit the van right where I'd been standing with a

Whiiiiiiillllllllllzzz**SPLATCH!**

It bounced into a nearby alley, flickering flames illuminating mossy stone walls like a strobing green torch, and SPLATCHing off a wheelie bin as it went.

There was a moment of silence, punctured after three seconds by a mournful 'toot'.

'What the heck was that?' I said from the ground.

'I don't know, it's most peculiar,' said Ishy. 'That doesn't normally happen until I've had my fifth can. It's the Jooce. Energy fart. Or, wait, you were talking about the weird green meteor, weren't you?' *Toot!* he added unhelpfully.

Chapter 2

SO WHAT'CHA WANT

I picked myself up.

'You OK?' said Ishy. 'You looked like you needed a push in the right direction.'

'Thanks, Ish,' I said. 'What the hecky hooha was that?'

'You should leave,' said the ice-cream man from inside his van. His voice carried authority, and he even looked quite authoritative in his traditional ice-cream-man uniform – white cap with blue peak, white tunic with blue piping on the shoulders.

'What? Should we?' I said.

'Yeah, look, I'll do you an ice cream, any flavour you want, for free, and then you should take it somewhere else.'

'Any flavour?' I said, my heart sinking a little.

'Yeah, you can even choose from the five luxury ones I've got in the back.'

'There are five more options?' I said, eyes widening.

'Oh no,' said Ishy.

'Five more options, yes,' said the ice-cream man.

I quickly did the maths. On a three-scoop cone that would be 25 times 3 times . . . ooooh dear. A bazilligillion combinations. My legs started wobbling a little. Maybe it was the narrow escape from nearly being SPLATCHED by a flying jelly comet; maybe it was the mathematical improbability that I would ever leave the hatch of this van with the exact right ice cream.

'Oh, deary me. You've bodged it. You just opened the door to a world of waiting for Leeza to choose,' said Ishy. 'You are going to be there for a while. So while she's choosing, do you reckon I could fish out whatever just bounced into that alley?'

'I don't think you should do that,' said the ice-cream man.

'That probably *is* what you think,' agreed Ishy, and he walked straight into the alley.

A hush descended. Was it my imagination or did the sun dip slightly but suddenly, lengthening the shadows around me as Ishy disappeared from view round the bend of the cobbled alleyway?

Yes. It was. But still.

We waited.

Silence. Even the gentle summer breeze seemed to hold its breath. I could hear the beating of my heart as it quickened.

Long, slow seconds ticked by. I couldn't bear the tension any more. I needed to know.

'What are the other five flav—' I started.

'Shush,' said the ice-cream man.

He was standing so still, the only movement

was a single bead of sweat winding its way down his face.

'Oh em actual gee, you should see this thing!' Ishy's voice echoed loudly from the alley. I smiled. He's such a goof!

'Oh, hello, what are *you* doing in here?' he said.

There was a hollow, plasticky clattering, like the sound a wheelie bin makes as it topples over twenty seconds after Ishy asks if you reckon he could jump over it.

And then silence again.

'He really shouldn't have gone in there,' said the ice-cream man.

'Why not?'

But before the ice-cream man could answer, a tall, middle-aged lady in jeans and a sensible anorak strode out of the alley and stood staring at me.

It was Mrs Ramshaw, the head of Owt School. It wasn't that unusual to see her emerging from an alley – she was a secret vaper. 'Secret' in the

16

sense that everyone knew she was a vaper because if she wasn't then how come she smelled like cake all the time? But for whatever reason she thought if she vaped in alleys, behind bike stands or in the stationery cupboard at school nobody would notice.

Mrs Ramshaw looked around, seemingly bewildered. She didn't quite look herself. Her face, with its ruddy cheeks, stern brow and shock of white frizzy hair, usually carried an expression somewhere between slightly miffed and fully dischuffed, so seeing her confused was a bit strange.

'Are you OK, miss?' I asked.

'I feel,' she said. 'I feel . . . I feel . . .'

She was starting to sound like a dance remix of herself.

And then her left arm lifted, then fell. And then her right arm did the same. She was holding her little pink vapeystick. She looked at it like she'd never seen it before, then she tossed it into a nearby bin.

'I feel...' Now she was rubbing her nose. 'Aaaaachooo!'

'I know that feeling,' I said.

A string of green goo stretched out of her left nostril briefly before snapping back in with an audible and gross FNAP.

'I have to go,' she said.

'OK,' I said.

'I have to get to school,' she said, looking round.

'It's Saturday evening, miss,' I said.

'No time to lose!' she said. And she started to walk.

I say walk; she was striding with immense purpose, ignoring me and the ice-cream man, and everyone else.

SHUNK!

The sound of the ice-cream man slamming his van hatch shut made me jump.

'Hey! I haven't chosen my ice cream!' I shouted, but I don't think the ice-cream man heard me as the back tyres of Daddy Cool screeched into life, spinning on the spot with a SQUEEEEEEE. And then off it shot, for around four metres before coming to a halt with a loud BANG.

'WHAT THE . . . ?' said the ice-cream man as he leapt out of his van.

'Hahaaaaaaa!' came the distinctive, cruel laugh of G-Dog from behind a nearby parked car.

'Who did this?' said the ice-cream man, pulling a blackened banana from the exhaust pipe of his van. 'That is SO ANNOYING! I'm gonna . . .'

I was just considering using this opportunity to order an ice cream – possibly banana flavoured now I thought about it – when he pulled out what looked like, but absolutely couldn't have been, a gun. It was big, and blue, and sparkly, and gun-shaped. He waved it around menacingly.

'WHEN I FIND OUT WHO . . . I'LL . . .' And then he seemed to catch himself. He looked at the thing which one hundred per cent could not have been a gun, then lowered it.

'It's fine!' he shouted. 'Funny joke. Didn't make me furious. Not one bit, actually.'

And he got back into his van and started it up again and managed to drive away quite slowly.

'That was weird, what I just saw in there,' said Ishy, emerging from the alley.

'I think the ice-cream man has a gun,' I said.

'OK, I need to recalibrate my definition of weird,' said Ishy. 'But what happened in the alley was definitely *odd*. Whatever landed in there it . . . I think it went up Mrs Ramshaw's nose.'

'HAHAAAAA! Did you see the look on his face? He was proper fuming!' G-Dog was doing a disjointed little victory jig in the middle of the road. I tried to ignore him. I had had a lot of practice at that.

'I think you might have had one too many Bubblejooces, Ishy.'

'Mmm. More likely I've had one too few,' said Ishy as he opened another can with a click-POOSh. 'Oh yeah, feel the boost!' he said between chugs.

20

I wasn't feeling a boost. I was feeling like I didn't have an ice cream. I was also feeling like something odd had definitely happened. I was also feeling a bit hungry. I had all the feels, as they say.

'Let's go!' said Ishy.

'OK!' I said. 'Where are we going?'

'Your place! Chish and fipps!' said Ishy, attempting to parkour over a small wall and failing spectacularly.

There we go, everything is back to normal, I thought – one hundred per cent wrongly as it turned out.

FLOOMCORP™

Medical professionals and influencers agree!
The number-one side effect of drinking deliciooos
FloomCorp Bubblejooce is

REFROOOSHMENT!

(Number four is farts.)

(Extract from *Galactic Scientooofic Research Journal*)

Chapter 3

HEAD OVER HEELS

The streets of Owt are wayward, wilful things.

I have been to towns where the streets seem to know exactly where they are going. They are all straight lines, even spacing and orderly junctions.

The streets of Owt get distracted and go exploring, heading up hills and down little dips, lined by higgledy stone walls, daydreaming themselves round mad little bends and detours. Sometimes three or four of them meet up for no real reason, crissing and crossing, playfully entwining before separating once more, each heading off in the general direction of wherever it is they are supposed to be going, in no particular hurry.

These were our streets.

They were streets for mooching along, drifting down, for wandering lonely as a cloud of sneeze-water.

Which is what we were doing, ambling in the general direction of home, our conversation meandering like the streets, probably taking up a bit more of the pavement than we should have, when there was a nervous cough from behind us.

'Er, sorry, excuse me, sorry, can I just . . . ?' came the voice of Miss Duffield.

She had been our teacher the year before and she was as jittery as a chicken.

My mum used to say she was one wobbly wheel away from a full breakdown, and while I wasn't quite sure what she meant there was always a look of fear in Miss Duffield's eyes. What she was scared of, I couldn't tell you.

Maybe she couldn't tell you either.

'Sorry, miss,' I said as we made room for her to get past.

'Sorry, thank you, sorry,' she said, and she skittered past us, head down, off round the long bend of The Longbend and maybe it was slightly our fault, maybe she would have been slightly further along the way if we hadn't slowed her down, but she was very much in the wrong place at the wrong time when there was a

WhiiiiiiiIIIIIIIIIIIZZZ**SPLATCH!**

A high-speed ball of flaming green jelly shot out of the sky and knocked her clean off her feet, through a hedge and into a garden.

I stood rooted to the spot. I knew I should probably do something but . . .

'Whoa!' said Ishy. 'What the . . .' He didn't even finish his sentence before he was racing off down the road and reaching into the hedge that Miss Duffield had just crashed through.

I was looking around again, silently pleading

25

for a grown-up to come and take charge of the situation, when Ishy dragged Miss Duffield out of the hedge with a leafy flourish. There were twigs and bits of flower stuck in her hair, but no sign of the green, gummy bullet that had taken her down.

'Miss, are you . . . ?' said Ishy.

'I'm fine, I'm fine. Everything is . . .'

And she lifted her left arm and looked at it like she'd never really noticed it before.

'Everything is . . .' she added, now inspecting her right arm like she'd found it in a charity shop and was checking it for scuffs. '. . . optimal,' she said.

And I was glad, of course I was, that everything was good, but I was also feeling weirdly sad and ashamed that I had just stood there. Maybe if she had lain in that garden for another couple of minutes I would have had time to spring into action. But instead I had done nothing.

Although, I mean, what was I *supposed* to do?

Something. I was supposed to do something,

I knew that.

I was so mired in a swirling cloud of guilt and shame and – hey, why not – pollen as well, I barely noticed the green gooey string swinging from Miss Duffield's nostril.

I did notice when she stuck out her tongue and used it to push the goo back up her nose. It was quite the move, almost impressive but also massively gross and very out of character for Miss Duffield, who I reckoned was the kind of person who if she sneezed into a tissue would never even open it up for a look afterwards to see what was what.

Then she looked around as though she'd forgotten where she was. She didn't really look OK.

'Are you OK?' said Ishy.

'I must . . .' she said, her head moving left to right and back like a boomeranged gif of a lighthouse. 'I just have to get to school.'

And then her head snapped to a standstill, looking straight ahead of her and she was off, stomping away down the hill with the same sense of clomping urgency that Mrs Ramshaw had shown earlier.

If anything she was a little more urgent, because Mr Croker had left his vintage Mini parked on the pavement towards the bottom of the hill, and rather than walk around it Miss Duffield just walked over it, which I can tell you now was very out of character for our old teacher, or any of our teachers really, or in fact anyone I'd met in Owt except maybe for Ishy but even he wouldn't have done it with Mr Croker staring at him, shocked, which is what he was doing right now as Miss Duffield stepped down from the bonnet of his vintage Mini and strode away.

'Oi!' he shouted after her.

She turned, and her face was ... different, somehow. She was smiling. She looked happy. No sign of stress, or worry, or tiredness. I say again – she was a teacher, so you can imagine how weird it was.

'The only way is up!' she said happily, before continuing down The Longbend on her way to school.

'Oh, man,' said Ishy. 'I think we need to adjust the weird scale again. What was that all about?'

'I don't know,' I said. 'Do you think we should tell someone?'

'Who? The police? The fire brigade? A car wash? And say what?' shrugged Ishy.

What would we say? Should we say anything? Was it our place to say anything? What exactly had happened anyway?

Ishy click-FOOShed another can of Jooce, and gluggglugglugged it in a noisily carefree way.

Which I suppose made the decision for me. If Ishy wasn't bothered, why should I be?

And that's why I didn't mention the flying green balls to anybody else that weekend. Maybe if I *had* told someone, we could have avoided an awful lot of unnecessary happiness and personal improvement but sadly it was not to be.

Chapter 4

OUR HOUSE

Mum was hanging wet clothes on the exercise bike in the hall.

'Oh, hello, Ishy. Staying for tea?' she said.

'If that's OK?' I said.

'Chish and fipps?' said Dad from the kitchen. This was his fish and chips joke and you could see how proud he was of it, like he was every time he made it, which was every time fish and chips was mentioned, which was around three times a week. He wandered into the hall, patting his belly, which visibly wibbled and rippled with every pat. 'The diet starts on Monday,' he said with a wink, like he did before every meal.

Every. Meal.

I forced my face to smile but inside I was cringing a little. My eyes flicked over to Ishy but he was just smiling like he was – I don't know – enjoying Dad's banter or something. It was very nice of him not to notice how embarrassing Dad was being.

The cringe was soon forgotten as I had bigger things to worry about. My brain started trying to work out what I might want from the chip shop. If you think the mathematics of ice-cream selection are tricky, imagine the calculations scrawled over the whiteboard of my mind when the equation includes scampi, sausages, fritters, beans, peas, gravy, curry sauce, fishcakes, and *three different kinds of battered fish*.

One day when I am grown up I will order the whole lot, served in a bucket with a pickled egg balanced on the rim – I assume every grown-up does this at some point in their lives because otherwise what's the point of growing up? But for now difficult choices had to be made.

To cut a very long story short, I had a battered fish of the third kind.

(The above sentence conceals a lot of ummming and aaaaahing and overthinking and making a decision and changing my mind and staring forlornly at the menu doing it all again but that is what cutting a long story short is all about.)

So I had fish and I ate it, and Ishy ate his chip butty with scraps, and Dad had his scampi, and Mum had her lightly battered haddock, and at one point Dad farted so loudly the windows practically rattled, and I was mortified and Mum giggled and Dad leaned over to me and Ishy and said, 'Rule number one, you've got to be yourself,' and Ishy high-fived him and said, 'Mr S, keeping it real!' and I wished a giant green jam-missile would strike my dad down because actually, no, don't be yourself, Dad, not if being yourself means farting loudly when we have guests, but then we watched some telly and

Ishy went home and everything was really normal and I do wish I'd enjoyed the whole, wonderful ordinariness of the night a bit more because everything was about to go completely and utterly *unprecedented*.

It started the next morning, when Mum decided to do some exercise.

Yeah, exactly.

'Tell your mum this isn't getting the clothes dry,' said Dad, who was sitting on the stairs as I came down.

I was not expecting to see this. Someone had cleared all the clothes off the exercise bike in the hall and put my mum on it. I mean, you'd think the most likely person to have done that would be my mum but that's because you don't know my mum very well.

And Mum smiled, the white of her teeth contrasting wildly with the shiny reddish-purple her face had gone and the lime green of the small bubble of snot she appeared to be blowing out of her left nostril. Her face was so colourful it resembled a sweaty rainbow.

'I have never felt better,' she said. 'I can feel them dolphins flowing!'

'Will you tell her, Leeza? She's knocked all the clothes off it. One minute she's going out the back to fill the bird feeder, and next thing she's back in the house pedalling like a maniac. She won't stop.'

'Five k!' said Mum, still smiling.

And she stopped.

'Well, thank goodness for . . .'

And Mum leapt off the bike, red-faced and panting, and jogged past me and out of the front door.

'Time me,' she shouted. And off she went down the path.

'I knew this would happen when she signed up to Mumsnet,' said Dad glumly. He patted his belly. 'This does not bode well. I foresee salads.' He put his head in his hands. 'Dinner should never be any more than one quarter green,' he sighed. 'It's not natural.'

Fifteen minutes later Mum jogged back into the house, huffing and puffing and grinning like a loon.

'Hoo! Wow, feel them dolphins,' she said. 'What's my time?'

'Er . . . well,' said Dad, looking at his watch. 'It looks like breakfast time to me but I could be wrong.'

'I asked you to time me, *Michael*,' said Mum, who was now lunging from left to right with her hands on her hips. 'I need to track my achievement.'

'I was a bit busy enjoying a scheduled meal and a discussion of the day with our daughter, *Sarah*,' said Dad.

We hadn't discussed anything, just eaten in silence.

I got a prickly feeling on the back of my neck, like some people get when an electrical storm is approaching, and like I get when Mum and Dad are winding themselves up, ready for an argument.

'It's endorphins, not dolphins,' I said, pushing my chair back from the table. 'I'm going out.'

And I left them to it.

Occasionally Mum and Dad would have a proper barnstormer of an argument, lots of shouting and saying 'Oh, I'm *sorry*,' without sounding sorry at all, and saying each other's names in italics and then there'd be two or three days of frosty words or, worse, frosty silences, and then things would be back to normal. It was all just part of the rhythm of our house, like Dad's fish and chips joke or Mum's firm putting down of her phone and promising not to look at it again that night before finding it back in her hand five minutes later. All this meant was that today would be tense, and that was fine because I'd be out with Ishy.

I say fine. I didn't like it. I just wished they could be more like everybody else, like the parents you'd see on the socials or burger adverts, all happy, smiling, fit, fashionable, pleasant to be around at all times. That would be brilliant, I thought.

As I left the house I heard a THWALTCH! sound and Mum saying, 'A bird's done its business on the window. Michael, would you go out and clean it up? I dunno what it's been eating but it's green.'

Chapter 5

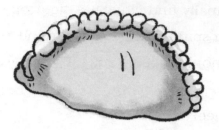

WISH YOU WERE HERE

I took my second-favourite route to the swingy park: up The Longbend, through Pig Alley to Finney's Walk, round the back of the library where it meets up with Finney's Other Walk and then left at The Rightway and there it was.

The swingy park had seen better days. It had two wobbly ladybird rides for the littlies, a roundabout, monkey bars, a scruffy seesaw and a set of swings with the chains wound tightly round the top bar so nobody could use them as was traditional on a Sunday morning. Still, it was a nice place to while away a sunny day, and this was a very sunny day.

I'd normally find Ishy here, tightrope-walking a fence or spinning round and round and round on the monkey bars, but he was nowhere to be seen.

'Ow, Sneezer!'

Great. No Ishy but a large slice of G-Dog, wafting a big stick around and obviously wanting to upset someone.

'Where's your fat boyfriend?' he said.

AAAAGH, I hated that! Ishy was NOT my boyfriend.

'He's not my boyfriend,' I said lamely.

'But he is fat,' said G-Dog, a mirthless grin plastered to his stupid face.

'He's . . .' I started. 'I mean, he's . . .'

'Fat,' said G-Dog. 'He's fat.' And he smiled again, looking pleased with himself.

Well, that was it.

'Listen, you ugly, stupid waste of space. Ishy could go on a diet tomorrow but you'll always be a moron with no friends because everybody

HATES YOU!'

Even as I said it I knew it was a horrible thing to say, but just for a moment, before he went back to being his normal belligerent self, just for one sweet moment G-Dog looked absolutely *devastated*, and just for a moment . . .

That felt good.

I turned and walked away, tutting, shaking my head, wishing once more that people, some people, could just be . . . *better* than they were.

Weirdly, at the time, I wasn't really including myself in that.

'He's a fatty fatty boom boom!' shouted G-Dog behind me, but I'd said all I wanted to and didn't look back.

By the time I had found Ishy in town, looking in the window of Owt's best – and only – pasty shop, I'd forgotten all about G-Dog.

'Where've you been?' I said.

'School,' he said.

'Haha, seriously though,' I said, because school would be the last place Ishy would be on a weekend.

'Honestly,' he continued. 'There is something proper unprecedented going on over there, you need to see it!'

'Mornin'. How's yer belly for spots?' said Mr Gofforth, who was the owner of Owt's best – and only – pasty shop. He was short, with close-cropped grey hair, a puffed-out chest and a back so straight you could iron shirts on it. His nose was pitted and cratered like a pink and red asteroid had crashed into his face.

'How's yer belly for spots?' is a real thing that people really say round here and yes it does get a bit annoying after around the fiftieth time you hear it in any given month but it's just a way for grown-ups to say 'How are you doing?' without sounding like they actually care about the answer.

To be clear, they absolutely *do not* want to inspect your belly to see if there are any spots on it, which is why Ishy had already lifted up his top.

41

'You tell me,' he said with a laugh.

'Put it away, for pity's sake, lad,' said Mr Gofforth. 'When I were your age I'd be out washing folk's cars or clearing their drives of a Sunday morning. Kids today,' he added with a shake of his head. 'Any road, can I tempt you to a pasty while yer loitering?'

Mr Gofforth made the best pasties, everyone said so. They were properly home-made, and you could taste the love and attention to detail that went into baking each one. Each filling was crafted using the best, locally sourced ingredients. The pastry would melt in your mouth, and then the flavours of the herby, spicy delights within would fill every corner of your mouth with savoury joy.

My mouth is practically watering even now, just thinking about them!

Unfortunately they were quite a bit more expensive than the equivalent from the supermarket so we never really bought any. We always loved walking past though, smelling the crisp, golden, buttery pastry and the range of delicious, hand-prepared fillings, on our way to buy a three-pack of limp cheesy-flavoured pastryish slices from the big shop.

'No, thank you,' I said with a smile.

'Yeah, thanks, but we're good,' said Ishy, tucking his shirt back in.

'No,' said Mr Gofforth. 'No, of course not. Silly me. Shame. Could be your last chance.'

And he sort of smiled, and sort of nodded his head, but neither gesture seemed as positive as they should have. He went back into his shop.

'We've got to go to school,' said Ishy. 'You've got to see what's happening up there.'

He ran off in the direction of school and I followed him because that's just the way weekends tended to go. We took a semi-short cut, over The Bumbles, up past What-the-Gate, and round Soggy Butt, which meant we approached the school grounds from Thitherfield to the rear of the hall.

Owt School was old-school. It was long and

flat-roofed and built with solid red-brick walls and grand, tall windows that had been painted shut many years ago. Over time it had grown almost organically: a new classroom added here, modern piping there, hut-like temporary classrooms dotted around the grounds. It was, above all else, definitely and totally and unmistakably a school. You could almost smell the chalk dust of centuries past in the air around it.

It *was* quiet, as you'd expect on a Sunday.

'Stop,' said Ishy. 'Look. The hall is full of teachers.'

'So? What are they doing in there?'

'Nothing,' said Ishy. 'Nothing at all.'

From where we stood I could see around ten teachers, and Ishy was right, they were doing nothing. About ten of them. They were just standing in a semicircle. They seemed to be wearing identical yellow clothes, but it was hard to tell from this distance.

'This is a bit— Whoa!' I was going to say 'weird'

but at that moment they had all jumped, once, in unison.

And then . . . nothing again.

'I'm going to take a closer look,' said Ishy, and before I could say anything, like 'Don't you dare!' or 'The heck you are!' he was off, running round to the other side of the hall, which meant he was out of sight.

I waited.

I waited for around five minutes.

Was it my imagination or did the sky darken slightly and a cold chill wind start to blow?

It was my imagination, yes, but it was all very eerie anyway.

And quiet. So quiet I could hear my heart beat, all weird and irregular and . . . oh, actually, no, that wasn't my heart beat, it was someone . . .

. . . or something . . .

behind me making weird booping and tushing noises.

Then:

'Put your hands in the air!' they said forcefully.

So I did. I put my hands up and awaited further instructions.

'And wave them around like you just don't care.'

What?

Chapter 6

WHERE IT'S AT

'Get up-ah, oh yeah' came the next instruction, and I thought, *I am up, aren't I?* Then: 'Get down!'

This was confusing.

I spun round to see G-Dog over by one of the temporary classrooms we had in the playground and he was acting very strangely indeed. He was looking at one arm like he'd never seen it before, then at the other, then moving them jerkily.

I gulped. It was very similar to what we'd seen Mrs Ramshaw and Miss Duffield doing after their encounters with the flying green meteors.

But he was also booping and tishing,

beatboxing with his mouth, badly, which as far as I knew the teachers weren't.

As far as I knew.

'Get down!' he said again, and I realised he was talking to himself.

Then he jerked like he'd been electrocuted, then he spun round and folded his arms and nodded his head, then he jumped, and spun again like . . .

Oh my! He was dancing! Urban dancing! Really, really badly. And he had a look on his face . . . a smile. A real, genuine smile. He was so into it, almost as though he didn't think what he was doing was the worst thing anyone had ever seen.

It was the worst thing I had ever seen. But he really looked like he was enjoying himself, and I was still feeling a bit guilty for yelling at him earlier, so I shouted, 'Nice moves!' and he stopped and looked up with an expression like I'd just caught him pooping in a plant pot or something equally bad and he shook his head and shouted, 'Oh, haha, shut up and leave me alone,' and he lumbered off across the field and I was only trying to be nice so what was all that about?

I felt a bit bad, then I remembered he'd been awful about Ishy so then I just thought *stuff him*, frankly.

Speaking of Ishy, where the heck had he got to? I turned back towards the hall and couldn't see the hall because all the teachers from the hall were standing in a line about two metres from me, and they were staring into space, not actually looking at me at all, *and how had they got there*, and they were all smiling and they were all wearing matching yellow tracksuits, and yellow trainers, and yellow headbands and they weren't moving or blinking, just staring into space and smiling and then suddenly . . .

they were looking . . .

right . . .

at . . .

me.

'Go home, Leeza, you're not ready for school yet,' said Mrs Ramshaw, who was in the middle of the row. She was smiling. 'You have to get ready for school.'

'I'm . . . er . . . I'm just waiting for Ishy,' I said.

'Ishy is getting ready for school,' said Mrs Ramshaw. 'He said he'd see you tomorrow.'

'Did he? But it's . . . it's Sunday morning,' I said.

'Big day tomorrow,' smiled Miss Duffield. 'Big day. Happy day,' she added.

'Go home and get ready for school,' smiled Mrs Ramshaw, and the whole line of teachers took a single step towards me. I took a step back.

This was very, very weird. Wasn't it? It's not just me, is it? This was properly unprecedented and I was all alone and I didn't know what else to do so I did what I was told. I turned and half walked, half ran across Thitherfield towards home. I looked back once, just as I reached the edge of the school grounds, and they were all still there, smiling at me. I shivered, despite the warm sunshine, and made my way home as quickly as Owt's streets would let me.

Home was almost as weird as school because it was empty, which it never was on a Sunday lunchtime. Normally Mum would be relaxing on the sofa with a book with a title like *The Girl in the Exciting Book*, while Dad would normally be cooking up an amazing, gravy-drenched dinner in the kitchen.

But they weren't. Weird.

I spread myself across the sofa, picked up the remote and started flicking through all the finest box sets available to humanity that afternoon. Occasionally one would catch my eye but as my thumb hovered over the OK button I'd wonder if I was really in the mood for another vampire rabbit anime, or a documentary about beauty pageants for American wizards, or a drama about a Korean ghost hospital, and actually I *wasn't* in the mood, I wasn't in the mood for *any* of it. So I kept on nudging through the list until I got hungry and padded into the kitchen.

I stared at the contents of the fridge for around

ten minutes but . . . well, you know what I'm like.
I closed the fridge and sighed. *Why am I like
this?* I thought.

THWALTCH!

Something hit the kitchen window.

It gave me such a shock I actually laughed
at myself, out loud, 'Ha!', and I ran over to the
window, which had a large, green goopy mess
the size of a paper plate in the middle of it.

It was disgusting.

It was . . .

Was it . . . ?

Was it bubbling?

I leaned in over the sink to get a closer look.

It was bubbling.

It was bubbling and . . .

Shrinking?

No, it was . . .

Un-splatting?

Slowly moving.

Like watching a green jelly baby melt, but in
reverse.

A shiver ran up my spine. Whatever it was, it shouldn't be doing that.

The shiver up my spine turned into a tickle in my nose.

Typical.

AH.

AH.

ATCHOO!

As everyone knows, it is impossible to sneeze and keep your eyes open at the same time.

I sneezed, I blinked, I unblinked; the gloop was gone.

Where had the gloop gone?

It must have just dropped or slid off the window, although it had left no trace that it was ever there.

I pushed my face even closer to the glass, to try and see where . . .

THWALTCH!

The window rattled and I staggered back from the sink, knocked into the table and fell to the floor. It had hit again, this time right where my face had been!

I sat, not breathing.

I was suddenly aware of the sound of something outside, pitter pitter pittering wetly.

Still I held my breath.

A familiar tickling started in my sinuses.

AH.

AH.

ATCHOO!

THWALTCH! rattattle

Where was that?

THWALTCH! rattattle

The front door! Something wet was banging at the front door, rattling the letterbox, and on an unrelated but similarly horrific note I had snot all over my chin like brave women in horror films never do.

THWALTCH! rattattle

I ran to the door and locked it, and put the chain on, and took two steps back and sank to the floor, and hugged my knees and held my breath again.

THWALTCH!rattattle

'Who is it?' I called.

No answer. My voice was croaky, my mouth dry, probably because I'd recently expelled all the liquid in my head out through my nose.

THWALTCH!rattattle

I fished for a tissue out of my pocket, wiped my chin, then grabbed my schnozzdongle from another pocket and switched it on. The two prongs glowed red, but before I could push them up into my nose I thought I heard a pitter pitter pittering, getting quieter. Further away.

Then . . .

There was no more banging.

No more pittering.

Silence.

Thank goodness.

I slowly raised my schnozzdongle to my face. I could feel another attack coming on.

THUD-DANG!

The door flew open with such force it BANGED off the wall, the letterbox RATATTLED wildly and the broken links of the door chain tinkled merrily to the floor.

I didn't scream; I was too busy sneezing like a cartoon dwarf.

Chapter 7

MANIC MONDAY

My parents stood at the door huffing, puffing and smiling.

'Whoa, did you see that?' huffed Dad. 'I knocked the door clean off its hinges.'

'You don't know your own strength,' smiled Mum. 'What's our time?'

Dad looked at his wrist, where he was wearing some kind of . . . some kind of fitness tracker.

'Blah blah blah something something something,' said my parents. I don't know what they were saying as they bustled into the house, all happy and sweaty.

I don't know what they were saying because I was concentrating on what they were wearing.

Brand-new yellow tracksuits, yellow trainers, yellow headbands.

What the hecky hooha was going on in this town?

'Something something something salad yum!' said Dad.

Salad. Dad was willingly, no, *happily* making a salad in the kitchen.

This was all too much. There was only one thing to do, and that was to just go up to my room for the rest of the day and pretend everything was normal.

I spent the evening flicking through the descriptions of lovely, happy cartoons on the streamers, staying away from the windows, listening to the almost constant whirring of the exercise bike's wheels downstairs and eating most of a jar of pickled onions I found in the back of the fridge on a brief expedition out of my room and past my parents, who were merrily doing press-ups in the living room.

Eventually I took myself to bed and I assume I must have fallen asleep at some point because the next morning I jolted awake with a start and checked my clock.

They didn't wake me up!

On a school morning, by the way. A Monday morning, which is the MOST school morning of all the school mornings.

Inexcusable!

They *knew*. They knew I never set my alarm. I could never decide whether to set it for the right time, or ten minutes early so I could have ten minutes' snooze, or twenty minutes early so I could have twenty minutes' snooze, or . . .

Too many choices. And that is why, when I woke up from a dream where I was trying to find a particular pair of socks in an overcrowded sock drawer while my bedroom slowly filled with green jelly, and I had exactly fifteen minutes to get from bed to school playground, I knew one thing for certain.

My day was ruined, right from the start, but it *wasn't my fault.*

Mum was supposed to wake me up.

This was her fault.

As I whizzed round the (empty, obvs; where were they?) house, tracking down socks, stuffing my schoolbag with books and the pickled-onion jar from last night (lunch), all with one hand while the other hand was brushing my teeth (no brush required: spot of toothpaste on forefinger; this was not my first school speed-run), it became crystal clear that this phase my parents were going through, all this self-improvement and maximising of potential, this loud and visible enjoyment of life, was going to have to stop before it ruined any more of my mornings.

I rocketed out of the front door with seven minutes to get to school. It would be a stretch but it was doable.

Are there any feelings greater than the feeling you get running like a powered-up hedgehog towards school on a Monday morning?

I mean, yes there are, one or two. I could list them but it would take up all the space in this book, space I need to tell you about how I became an ice-cream man, so I won't list them but I think the short answer is 'nearly all the feelings are better than that one particular feeling'.

The way to school took me up Pig Alley, along the Wobbly Cobbles, through the town centre, past the swingy park, over the Trolley Beck and . . .

Whoa, back up there a minute.

The swingy park was surrounded by cones. Next to it was a sign reading 'Opening soon – the Arena of Achievement brought to you by FLOOMCORP™. *The future is now*'.

Next to the sign was Mr Gofforth. He was smiling, which was odd.

'What are they doing with the park?' I huffed, looking at my watch. I figured I had around twenty-five seconds to spare for this very important conversation.

'State-of-the-art fitness park,' smiled Mr Gofforth.

Normally Mr Gofforth would have been full of fury about another outside business setting up in Owt. He was constantly moaning about the supermarket, for example.

'You can't build a fitness park in a day,' I said.

'Not with that attitude you can't,' said Mr Gofforth, shaking his head.

'What? What's attitude got to do with—'

'You're not ready for school,' he said, and he smiled at me again and I took an involuntary step back because there was something chilling and wrong about that smile.

'Now, get yourself to school. It's very important, is school. It sets you up for your future. And you don't have long, cos the future is now.' He tapped the sign with a chuckle.

I set off again, dimly aware that Mr Gofforth hadn't even asked how my belly was for spots. It was a strange time all round.

I reached the school playground just as the bell rang for us all to line up and go in. I had achieved school!

I don't love school, not particularly. But school is something that happens to me, regularly, and it has precisely this going for it: I know where I am with school, because I am wherever school tells me to be, with whoever school tells me to be with, doing whatever school tells me to do. It has timetables, and set expectations, and rules, and a syllabus, and bells, and if you play your cards right you don't have to make a single decision all day and what's not to like about that?

So where the hecky slam was everybody? No parents at the gates. No kids lining up in the yard. The bell was ringing, but there was only Charlotte Actually, standing alone in the playground, looking as confused as I was feeling, only more so because she was better at doing everything than I was.

'Seen this?' she said, pointing at the signage that Owt School displayed like a name badge, kind of 'Hi, I'm Owt School. Nice to meet you!'

Only the sign didn't say 'Owt School', it said 'Owt Academy of Winners and Winning' and there was something very, very scary about that. I did not like the sound of it one little bit.

And I really didn't like it when Mr Lowe strode out of the doors to reception, pointed at me, opened his mouth and screamed.

Chapter 8

SHAME SHAME SHAME

'Eeeeeeeeeeeeeeeeeeeeeeeeeeeeeeeeeeeeeeeee,'
went Mr Lowe.

My stomach turned as cold as ice cream and
my legs went to jelly. All I'd need was a cherry
on my head and I would be the full knickerbocker
glory of fear.

All I ask of school is that I stay invisible. I do
what you tell me to do, just don't single me
out, don't tell me off, don't call attention to
me, and definitely, *definitely* don't point at me
and scream.

I honestly didn't know what to do. My eyes

were starting to prickle and it wasn't an allergic response, unless I was allergic to full-fat creepy weirdness.

That's when Mrs Ramshaw emerged from the school with a smile. She was wearing a bright-yellow tracksuit accessorised with a yellow towelling sweatband, and she jogged up to Mr Lowe and smacked him in the head with the heel of her palm.

'Eeee eee eeeeee,' went Mr Lowe, slightly quieter, and his eyes started rolling like lemons in a fruit machine.

Wallop! She smacked him again.

And Mr Lowe sort of wound down like when one of those yappy, somersaulting dogs runs out of batteries. He bent over at the waist, arms hanging low, swinging slightly in the breeze.

There was a quiet moment when I was looking at Mrs Ramshaw, who was smiling at me.

And then he wound slowly back to life, eyes normal, smiling away.

'EeeeeeEEEEEIIIIIIIIIIiiiiiiiiiiiii-in you come, in

you come, in you come, we've been doing maxercises for the last half-hour!'

'Come on, no dawdling,' said Mrs Ramshaw.

And before I knew it my feet were obeying the teachers because that's what I do – I was already halfway to the entrance when Charlotte piped up.

'Excuse me, miss, but I was here on time. How come everyone's been here for half an hour already? I don't get it.'

I would say I rolled my eyes at that, but after what Mr Lowe's eyes had just been up to I didn't bother, so I just shook my head a little and thought, *Don't make a fuss, Charlotte, that is such a schoolboy error. If you make a fuss then they will take notice of you and then where will you be? Just do what you're told – reluctantly, badly if you must – but do it quietly.*

Or should I say . . . *look* like you're doing what you're told.

I had walked obediently past Mrs Ramshaw and Mr Lowe, heading for the door, and they were now beautifully distracted by Charlotte piping up like an amateur, and I stopped and looked at the doors and I thought *nope*.

Nope nope nope.

Everything was really super-unprecedented and do you know what? There was no way in the world I was going into that school. Not a chance. Are you kidding me? What, do you think I'm an idiot?

I started to run. I didn't know where I was running to, I just knew what I was running *from*, which was this school in general and Mrs Ramshaw in particular because she was properly freaking me out.

I was running past the big hall windows when I realised the big hall windows meant that whoever might be in there would be able to see me but hopefully nobody would be in there but I sneaked a quick look and *everybody* was in there so whoops.

The whole school, by the looks. All dressed in yellow.

I dropped to the ground, beneath the windows, and stayed there for a bit.

Now what?

I wasn't very good at this.

I thought I could hear the pounding of my heart in my ears but it turned out it wasn't my heart at all.

It was the STAMP STAMP STAMP of a hundred feet tramping in unison in the hall.

And then the chanting started.

Usually when we had assembly in the hall, the first thing we'd do is sing the school song. It's a catchy little number about friendship, and happiness, and trying our best.

But that's not what I could hear from the hall. They weren't singing, they were chanting. It was muffled but it was loud enough to hear the words and what they were chanting was:

Up! Up! Up! We're reaching for the sky!
The only way is up! And that's our battle cry!
Achieving in the morning

While other kids are snoring
Don't stop to smell the roses, that's a stupid
waste of time!

I mean, quite apart from being weird it was factually inaccurate. Anyone who thinks the only way is up shouldn't get a job as an airline pilot, for example.

In fairness I could totally get behind the not-smelling-roses thing, but that was because rose pollen made my nose run like the unlimited Bubblejooce pump at our local PeriPeriPeriPeri restaurant. Having said that, I wouldn't go round chanting about it like it was some sort of rule. What the heck was going on? If you want to sniff a rose, knock yourself out, don't mind me. More pollen up your nose means less up mine.

I slowly popped my head up to the window and peered in. I could see them. All of them. My friends, foes, classmates, playground faces. All of them were dressed head to foot in bright-yellow tracksuits. All of them wearing fetching yellow towelling headbands, and each of them stepping up on to, and then down from, the wooden blocks in front of them.

Every time they chanted 'Up, up, up, we're reaching for the sky,' that's exactly what they did, arms outstretched, rigid in the air, palms facing the ceiling.

It was like a robot's version of doing 'YMCA' at a wedding.

It made me feel strange. My fingertips tingled. There was an odd buzz, not audible, just an energy in the air, like the atmosphere itself was agitated.

I was agitated, that's for sure.

And there in the middle of it all, totally joining in obediently, not taking the micky or smiling, was Ishy.

I sank to the ground again.

Ishy was in there and I was out here and that was just going to have to change one way or another.

I sighed. Before we were both out here, we

were both going to have to be in there.

What a shame. I didn't want to go in there. Really I didn't. But I didn't have a choice, did I? I had to get Ishy.

So I ran back round to the front of the school and walked right in like an idiot.

ANNOUNCE NEW FACTORY

The Floom Corporation are pleased to announce the opening of a new Happinish™ processing plant with the creation of 6,000 new jobs. 'Of course, each employee will have their own company vehicle – that's the FloomCorp way!' said Floom's outspoken CEO, Noblong Floom. 'And yes, the vehicles will be eco-friendly. All models emit some carbon dioxide, and some are known to emit methane – but nowhere near me or anyone I know and that's got to be good news!'

(FloomCorp Press Release, reprinted in
The Financioool Tooomes)

Chapter 9

JUMP AROUND

The corridor had been redecorated. It was covered in posters letting us all know THE FUTURE IS NOW and also that we should DRINK BUBBLEJOOCE FOR A BURSTY BOOST. Each one had the words 'The Academy of Winners and Winning is TM & © FloomCorp'.

'Huh,' I said aloud. I had always hoped the future would have been all about jetpacks and world peace, not soft drinks. I kept walking.

What now? Ishy had been in the hall. Everyone was in the hall. It seemed like a very bad idea therefore to go to the hall but I say again: Ishy was in the hall so that's where I would have to go.

I sneaked up to the hall door and was about to do some really excellent 'spying through the window and making a plan' when the whole idea of spying and planning became irrelevant because the door opened to reveal Miss Bean.

'Join us,' she smiled.

In more precedented times, like last Friday and every other day until today, Miss Bean was a symphony of grey. Grey clothes, grey face, grey outlook, like a slow-moving cloud of drizzle. I had literally never once seen Miss Bean smile. One time I did see her almost grinning but it turned out her face was twitching due to a build-up of static electricity caused by a combination of all the grey wool she was wearing, plus the friction of her foot-dragging as she trudged towards another mirthless lesson.

And now here she was, dressed head to toe in sunny yellow, beaming like a presenter on Saturday morning TV.

What was happening here?

I strained to see past her, looking for Ishy. Ishy, who would in normal times be stood at the back of the hall with me, having a chortle and making jokes about the nonsense song with its nonsense words and these nonsense clothes everyone was wearing,

It took a moment, but yes, there he was. Ishy was tramping up on to his block and down from his block, a beatific smile on his face, chanting with the rest of them and apparently not even changing any of the words to 'bum' or 'poop' or other, better words. Something was very wrong here.

'Join us,' smiled Miss Bean again, and she held the door wider.

'Er . . . I'd rather not,' I said.

'Leeza,' smiled Miss Bean. 'Please, come in and maxercise with us.'

Oh, heck! What was I supposed to do now? I had utterly failed to rescue Ishy. I needed help.

'Wait,' smiled Miss Bean, her eyes narrowing.

'Are you ready for school? I don't think you're ready for school. Come with me and we'll get you ready for school.'

'No, thank you,' I said quietly to myself, because who was around to hear it?

'You heard her,' said a voice from behind me. 'She said no.'

'I did,' I agreed, nodding, then turned to see who it was.

Charlotte Actually to the rescue!

'And now we're leaving,' said Charlotte Actually.

'We are,' I nodded. 'Are we?' I added, because *were* we? We were in school, on a school day. Where were we supposed to go?

'No,' smiled Miss Bean. 'No, you're not.' And she turned to the hall full of kids and said, 'Get them.'

Whoa.

You know that feeling?

When someone, completely unexpectedly and out of the blue, instructs around a hundred people to 'get' you?

No?

Well, let me tell you there's no feeling like it.

And if a hundred kids had started running towards us at that point, that would have been horrible enough. But that's not what happened.

What happened was this:

Everyone stopped stomping and turned to face us.

Their faces, so happy and smiling up to that point, slackened, all expression gone.

Their eyes rolled like the digits on a timer app.

And then from each of their left nostrils, a small green gooey balloon squooged.

BaloOOOOOOOOOOOOOOOO*FLOPP*

One hundred translucent green flubber balls flurped out of the nose holes in one hundred red, sweaty faces and flatched to the floor and it was exactly as disgusting as it sounds. More, actually.

And then each of the gooballs formed into the shape of a half-formed person, with stumpy little arms and stumpy little legs.

They were about ten centimetres high, and each one took a small, gummy step towards us, and then another and then . . .

Pitter pitter pitter pitter

The sound of two hundred sticky little feet jogging towards us. I backed away slowly. Too slowly probably, but my brain and body were so fizzy with adrenalin I didn't know what I was doing.

Charlotte hadn't moved from the spot. She was . . . crouching. Tensing. She almost looked like she was ready for a fight, which seemed kind of silly to me.

I put my arm on her shoulder to drag her away when . . .

'Are you kidding me?' cried Miss Bean.

I mean, *quite*. I was just about to say something similar.

'Not on foot, you idiots! Get back in the machines and GET THEM!' she cried.

I really wished she would stop saying 'Get

them!' It was properly freaking me out.

I watched as one hundred little green jelly men leapt high into the air and flew back into the nose holes of one hundred slack-jawed kids, whose eyes stopped rolling and smiles returned like they'd just hit the jackpot. One hundred pairs of eyes fixed on us with an audible 'Oh *no*'.

Actually the audible 'oh no' was me, because oh no, you know?

Chapter 10

RACE FOR THE PRIZE

'Run!' said one of us; it's not important which.

OK, it was Charlotte, but I was definitely just about to say it, it's just she got in there first, which was typical Charlotte, actually.

Although on the other hand maybe we could have tried to talk to them. They were our friends and classmates, after all. I mean, OK, they seemed to be possessed by gooey little jelly men but maybe they would have seen reaso—

Anyway, we ran.

Off down the corridor as fast as we could go. Or as fast as I could go. Charlotte did running club so she was definitely holding back, keeping her pace so she was just in front of me, which was very nice of her, actually.

We kept running.

I don't know about Charlotte but in that moment all I could think about was getting out of school. All my other worries and concerns, all the mad confusing swirl of nonsense that would normally be cluttering my head, had cleared. In some ways it was nice.

In most ways, of course, it was the most horrible thing that had ever happened to me.

We were so nearly out, we could see the light streaming in through the glass panels in the school's front doors, when that light was blocked by a shadow in the shape of Mrs Ramshaw, because that's who was suddenly standing between us and escape.

Well, that was it. We were stuck in school and we were just going to find out what *getting got* meant and there was nothing we could do about it. I started to slow down but Charlotte Actually . . .

actually . . .

. . . sped up, dropped to the floor and slid the final few metres between her and Mrs Ramshaw and she . . .

. . . swept Mrs Ramshaw's feet from under her . . .

And Mrs Ramshaw clattered to the ground while Charlotte Actually sprang back to her feet and took a corner leading away from the front door. I could see Mr Lowe was standing guard in the playground so that was probably the right decision.

My mum would sometimes ask, 'If Ishy jumped off a cliff would you follow him?' and my answer would usually be 'Probably not' but Charlotte just ran into the stationery cupboard and I totally followed her, so who knows.

She slammed the door behind us. We were in a very small space, surrounded by boxes of pencils and erasers, piles of papers and books, and the unmistakable vanilla smell of Mrs Ramshaw's 'secret' vapey breaks.

'OK, we only have a minute. Here's the thing, Leeza,' she said. I could barely hear her over the pumping of my heart babooming in my ears. 'There is something very strange going on here and I need you to hide in this cupboard while I find out what it is, and hopefully put a stop to it.'

'OK,' I said. It seemed reasonable enough.

'There's a hatch up there,' she said, pointing at some sort of trapdoor in the ceiling of the cupboard. 'I can lift you; can you get in there?'

'I think . . . Yes . . .' I said, and she gave me a boost up and yes, I could lift the hatch and climb into what seemed like an attic for tiny people. It was the space between the classrooms and the roof. I found I could move around OK as long as I stayed crouching. All the while, Charlotte was speaking clearly and with purpose.

'I feel like I've been training all my life for this, Sneezer,' she said. 'Karate club, judo club, running club, climbing club. I am at my physical and mental peak at age twelve. They don't know who they're messing with.'

She sounds so heroic, I thought, crouching in my loft hole. *Because she's a hero. What am I? Some kind of loft-hobbit.*

'I'm going to go out there and I'm going to sort this out, and if anybody tries to stop me then I'm very much afraid I'll have to—'

It was a very stirring speech and it was clearly leading up to some kind of climax. Which meant it was a real pity that the cupboard door was suddenly splintered in ten different places by the hands and arms of the enemy.

No, of our friends.

No, of . . . of the . . .

. . . of our school friends, moving around under the control of those little gummy creatures.

They were being driven. The children, the teachers, they were being driven by these things, like they were lorries, or machines in a factory.

Charlotte was yanked bodily from the cupboard by the grasping hands of the Driven,

86

and that was the end of her speech, and her plan too.

And also, seeing as the hero was now being dragged down the corridor towards some sort of fate, leaving her sidekick quietly cowering in a dark crawl space, not really wanting to leave, like, *ever*, it looked as if it might be the end of the book on top of everything else, which, given that there were supposed to be another twenty chapters or so, was an absolute catastrophe.

Chapter 11

JUST LIKE CHRISTMAS

I sat quietly in my high hidey-hole.

I didn't want to make any noise in case the Driven came and got me. I did not want to get got.

I whiled away ten or fifteen seconds calculating how long I would be able to stay up here, given I had no water and a jar with five small pickled onions to sustain me.

If I was to eat one pickled onion every three days then . . .

I was doomed.

I was in more of a pickle than the onions

were, that's for sure.

And then I felt sad and wished my dad was here because that's exactly the kind of joke he would have made, and I would have groaned and rolled my eyes and quietly loved him for it. My eyes started to prickle and so did my nose but we have to remember I am allergic to things and I *definitely* wasn't going to cry.

I heard the voice of Mrs Ramshaw in the cupboard beneath me.

'Can you feel it, in the air?'

If she was talking about emotion, I thought, then yes, and I could feel it in my nostrils. My dad was getting up my nose again. Aagh, another Dad joke!

'I can, I can. It crackles,' said Mr Lowe.

My eyes were watering. I was trying to concentrate on what they were saying. I'd felt that crackling too, a weird energy in the air. What was it?

'It is ready for harvesting. Are we ready to begin processing the children?'

I needed to hold this sneeze in for as long as I could. They were *processing children*?

'The canisters are primed and ready for filling. We will begin processing immediately.'

I could feel the sneeze creeping up the back of my nose. *Processing?* Processing didn't sound very nice. I knew what processed cheese looked and tasted like. It's all right, in its way and in its place, sitting wetly on a dirty burger, but it is flat and uniform and plasticky and an unnaturally bright-orange colour in exactly the way that actual cheese isn't.

What the heck would processed children look like?

'Ah!' I said. Oh no.

And beneath me:

Nothing said Mrs Ramshaw.

Nothing said Mr Lowe.

'AH!' I said.

Nothing said Mrs Ramshaw

'What?' said Mr Lowe. 'What, up there? Oh, sorry,' he added, then whispered, 'Up there?'

'YES, UP THERE,' bellowed Mrs Ramshaw. 'You are such an idiot. You are clearly operating at optimal levels of being an idiot. You have maximised your potential for idiocy. Well done, Mr Lowe. You represent one hundred per cent of my recommended daily allowance of vitamin idiot. Get up there, get whoever it is and then report back to me for the maxercise you clearly need.'

'AAAAATCHOOOOO!' I said, and then I scrambled away from the hatch, which was cracking open.

I stuffed the glowing schnozzdongle up my hooter, hoping it would prevent any further noisy outbursts, then looked around desperately for an escape route.

The crawl space I was in led off into darkness. But where else could I go?

Thankfully, the schnozzdongle was working and my red nose was lighting the way.

It meant I could see about thirty centimetres in front of my face as I scurried on my hands and knees, past old, battered boxes of old, battered books, terrified out of my mind but also strangely comforted by the song that had started playing on a loop in my head. You probably know the song, about a useful animal with a lighty-up red nose. It's sung by happy children in December every year but it's also owned by a big, powerful corporation with very keen lawyers and it's very expensive to write it down in a book so I won't.

But you know the song I mean.

I passed a box filled with tinsel and long, scruffy paper chains.

The ground under me seemed a bit bouncy. Less than solid. Owt School was old, and bits of it were always peeling away or falling off. This really wasn't safe, but I could hear Mr Lowe crawling behind me so what other choice did I have?

No choice.

Keep crawling.

I passed a sign saying 'To the roof' next to a

short ladder leading to another trapdoor. *Maybe I should go up there*, I thought. But then I'd be absolutely trapped. I kept on crawling.

I passed five shiny metal canisters, each one the size of a soft drinks vending machine, each one marked with the word 'HAPPINISH'.

What the heck was happinish? It sounded like someone didn't know how to spell 'happiness'.

CRACK

Part of the floor beneath my left knee fell away, and bright, artificial light streamed into the crawl space through the hole it made.

I was crawling on polystyrene. These were the ceiling tiles of the classroom below.

Dimly, ahead of me I could see another trapdoor set in the floor, lit up in red by my nose so bright.

If I could just make it to . . .

Oh no, it was rattling. Someone was trying to push it open.

I shuffled around, still on all fours. I couldn't see Mr Lowe, but I could hear him crawling stealthily towards me. The sounds of his huffing and puffing were oddly deadened by all the boxes and dust.

I turned back. The trapdoor was still rattling. Maybe if I was fast I could hide or . . . I fumbled with my schnozzdongle – I needed to switch it off if I wanted to get away.

And then Mrs Ramshaw crashed her head through the thin wood of the closed trapdoor with a . . . well, with a CRASH!

'Hello,' she smiled, hair covered in splintered plywood.

'Hi,' I said. I couldn't help it! That's what you say when someone says hello to you! 'How's your belly for spots?' I added, playing for time as I looked around. Was there any other way out?

'What?' said Mrs Ramshaw, her brow furrowing. 'Spots? What are you talking about?'

I couldn't go forwards and I couldn't go backwards.

I was out of choices. There was only one way to go.

Like the new school song said: 'The only way is up'.

I kicked my foot down hard, smashing the polystyrene tiles beneath me, and down I went.

Chapter 12

JUST DROPPED IN

I landed with a thump in the middle of room 2c, where normally at this time on a Monday morning me and Ishy and all our chums, foes and assorted classroom-fillers would be sitting in rows learning about King Humphrey the Tenteenth and his too many wives.

History was not happening in room 2c this morning. Which was partially a relief – as I'd not done the weekend reading – but also partially a bit weird. The room was empty. Of everything. No books. No wall friezes. No chairs. No . . . You get the idea.

It wasn't a room any more, it was an empty box.

It was dark – the blinds were down. Polystyrene drifted slowly and silently from the hole I had made in the ceiling, landing on my shoulders like snow. My nose prickled because, yes I am allergic to polystyrene – of course I am. I switched my dongle back on because I didn't need any sneezy distractions just now.

I briefly felt Christmassy, in the same way that a turkey does.

OK.

I was in here. *They* were up there. But they could easily come down here – I had just made a big hole in the ceiling.

I needed to get out of here, and quick.

I had two options. The door or the window.

Door or window.

So which was it to be? The door, which would be easiest, probably, but would just lead me back towards the hall and all my Driven chums. Or the window: riskier – it might well be locked, and they didn't open very wide, but if I could get through I'd be out.

Door. Or window.

I don't know how much time passed. Could have been seconds; could have been days.

'You confuse me,' said a voice from above.

Made sense. I confuse myself a lot of the time.

'Why have you not tried to leave the room?' It was Mrs Ramshaw, of course, her head sticking through the hole in the ceiling, gazing down at me.

'I *am* trying!' I said. 'I just don't know whether to go through the door or the window!'

Which was just *brilliant* of me. I knew that Charlotte Actually would never tell the enemy what her plans were, but I couldn't help myself.

'You couldn't give me another few minutes, could you?' I asked hopefully. 'It would really help me out.'

Mrs Ramshaw smiled.

'Oh dear, I can do better than that. I can take

away all your doubt, your confusion, your anxiety. I can make it so you'll never worry about making a decision ever again. Because you'll know exactly what you want, and you'll know exactly how to get it. And it will be the same thing every single day. How does that sound?'

That sounded . . .

Horrifying.

That wasn't what I wanted at all, was it?

How would that help?

'All you have to do is help me help you. Open your mind,' she said. 'And your nostril; that will help too.'

And then she did a disgusting thing that I've seen Dad do on occasion, and when he does it he at least has the good grace to look disgusted with himself, but Mrs Ramshaw just looked serene and pleased as she closed one of her nostrils with a finger, and blew, hard.

An apple-sized blob of green goo flew out of her other nostril . . .

right . . .

at . . .

my . . .

face

(which, to be fair to Dad, he would never do).

I scrambled back fast, so fast I slipped and fell on to my backside as the green goo schplotted on to the wooden floor in front of me.

'You get ready for school and I'll be down in a minute to take you to the hall,' smiled Mrs Ramshaw from the ceiling. 'And the good news is, going to the hall is all you will want to do at that moment. You can thank me later.'

Her head disappeared back into the ceiling. I probably had about a minute before she was down here.

The green blob wobbled and stretched, forming little arm shapes and leg shapes. It stood and shook itself like a self-wobbling jelly, and then it took a step towards me.

I scootched myself back along the floor, like a dog with an itchy bum.

It took another step, and then it seemed to shrink, compressing itself down like . . . like a spring getting ready to

SPROING

It launched itself at my face. I had scootched myself all the way to the wall. I had nowhere to go.

Everything went in slow motion. And in slow motion it looked like the green, translucent snotmonster was hovering in the air and slowly expanding. But it wasn't getting bigger, it was getting closer . . .

to . . .

my . . .

face . . .

And its gooey green arms were slowly reaching out for me, like it wanted to hug me.

And still it got bigger. Still it got closer.

Until it practically filled my vision with greenness.

Although . . . I noticed the closer it got the more the green was tinged with shimmering red highlights.

Quite Christmassy again, I thought, because I cannot stay on topic.

It was the red light of my schnozzdongle, of course.

The gummy thing was WAY TOO CLOSE NOW, but something happened. It flattened in mid-air, like it had hit an invisible wall, and then it just flopped to the floor by my feet.

We both sat for a bit, neither of us moving.

OK, if I was going to do something, now was the time. Mrs Ramshaw would be in any second.

I rose, slowly, so as not to startle the creature.

I needed to trap it but the room was empty.

I reached into my schoolbag and fished out my lunch – the jar of pickled onions. I quickly unscrewed the lid and chucked the contents out on to the floor. Then I moved ever so slowly towards the gummy thing and held the jar over it.

It was a very similar skillset to when I have

to coax a spider from the living room into a glass because Mum's lost her chill completely and wants to set fire to the room and move house and Dad wants to prove he's some sort of mighty superhero by smacking it to bits with a shoe.

I swept the gummy man into the jar, and slapped on and screwed the lid just as the door opened and Mrs Ramshaw walked in. She turned and produced a key, locking the door behind her. We were trapped.

Mrs Ramshaw moved purposefully towards me. She smiled as she moved, and then she flew feet first into the air . . .

Oh my gosh, I thought, *THEY CAN FLY!?* This changed everythi—

O . . . h, wait, no . . .

. . . because she then fell and landed on her back with a thwumping noise so awful I almost felt winded myself. As she landed a green blob flew out of her nose and splatched on the far wall.

Whoops.

She'd slipped over on the pile of pickled onions, once again proving that the only way was definitely not 'up'.

Chapter 13

CAN'T GET YOU OUT OF MY HEAD

'Ooh, ow!' said Mrs Ramshaw. 'Oh, my back! What's . . . what's going on? Leeza, could you help . . . ow!'

Oh gosh, this was awkward.

Was I supposed to apologise, or what?

I knew then, and I still know now, that violence is not supposed to solve anything. But at that moment it did rather seem that I had inadvertently and violently knocked something bad out of Mrs Ramshaw's head.

So . . . yay me?

'What on earth is that?' shrieked Mrs Ramshaw.

'Whatever it is it's banned from this school!'

The jelly man had unstuck itself from the wall and was moving slowly but surely along Mrs Ramshaw's leg.

'Getitoffme! Ow, my back!'

I'd really hurt Mrs Ramshaw, and it didn't seem to have caused the jelly man too much inconvenience.

So violence *had* worked, but only for around thirty seconds.

The jar I was holding kicked, as if to remind me I had my own problems to deal with. My captive jelly man was frantically boinging and squidging from side to side, trying to escape.

I put the jar into my bag, because what was I supposed to do with it? Why did I do this? It was like trapping a wasp under a glass – how was I going to release it without getting stung? Or was I just going to keep it in there until . . . until . . .

I didn't know what the heck my plan was.

AND THIS IS WHY I DON'T LIKE MAKING DECISIONS. YOU MAKE ONE DECISION AND,

OH, LOOK, NOW IT'S TIME TO MAKE ANOTHER ONE.

It's relentless and it's tiring, and I was already fed up with it and I knew I would likely have to make another couple of choices before the day was done, which frankly sucked. I needed to find someone to take charge and help me get through this.

Ishy. I needed Ishy.

When I saw him I would . . . I would . . .

I would knock the bad thing out of his head and get him and me the heck out of here.

Plan.

The jelly man was scrambling across Mrs Ramshaw's stomach now.

It was really scary, and what made it worse was the soundtrack. Was it my imagination or could I hear weird, out-of-key chimes playing a mournful and creepy tune?

No, it was not my imagination. There was an ice-cream van somewhere in the vicinity. *Good luck selling any ice creams today*, I thought.

'Get it off meeeeeeee!' wailed Mrs Ramshaw, reminding me not to think about ice cream for at least the next five minutes.

I was just about to help her, probably, when the hairs on the back of my neck stood on end – there was something happening behind me.

I turned. Some sort of shiny silver snake was dangling from the ceiling. It was made of coiled metal, and it slinked and crackled with some kind of invisible energy as it moved. It snaked through the air towards me and, I'm sorry, but me and room 2c were absolutely done at that point.

I was just about to run out of the room when the windows furthest from me went KRA-SHATTER and two uniformed figures jumped in, knocking blinds and shards of glass everywhere. They landed, rolled and sproinged back to their feet with a synchronised 'Huh!'

OH, THANK GOODNESS IT WAS THE ARMY!

No, wait. Wrong uniform.

OH, THANK GOODNESS IT WAS THE POLICE!

Ah . . . no. Wrong uniform. They were wearing peaked caps. White tunics. Blue piping here and there.

OH, THANK GOODNESS . . . IS IT THE COASTGUARD MAYBE?

No, not the coastguard, or the police, or the army, or the Justice League or even Paw Patrol. No, I recognised that uniform.

Oh. Thank goodness. It was two ice-cream men.

What?

DO YOU HAVE WHAT IT TAKES TO BE AN ICE-CREAM MAN?

DO YOU KNOW YOUR SPRINKLES FROM YOUR CRUSHED NUTS?

DO YOU KNOW YOUR FLAKE FROM YOUR FUDGE FLURRY?

DO YOU KNOW YOUR EVERYDAY FLYING SAUCER FROM YOUR KROLLIAN SPACE CRUISER IN FULL ATTACK MODE?

HOW'S YOUR AIM?

(From a job advertisement placed in a weird little corner of the Internet)

Chapter 14

SHOULD I STAY OR SHOULD I GO?

One of the ice-cream men shouted 'Freeze!', which was the kind of thing Dad would have found funny. He'd say . . . 'Ice-cream men . . . freeze, get it!?' And it would have been a bit funny but I wouldn't have allowed my face to smile because I don't know a good thing until it's gone.

The ice-cream men pointed their guns at Mrs Ramshaw.

WAIT – THEY HAD GUNS?

Yes, they did, and I had seen one earlier, in Chapter Two, remember? Their guns were blue and sparkly and kind of fun-looking but they were unmistakably guns with triggers and telescopic sights and shooty ends and they were pointing the shooty ends right at Mrs Ramshaw, which didn't seem right, and before I knew it I was standing between them and her and I was saying 'Stop, don't shoot', which is something I never thought I would ever have to say.

I quickly turned to check on Mrs Ramshaw just in time to see the jelly man shlurp back up her nose.

Uh oh. I looked back at the ice-cream men.

'You can't shoot her! There's something in her head that shouldn't be there!' I said. 'She's being Driven.'

'It's all right, come here,' said the taller of the ice-cream men, holding out a blue-gloved hand. 'We need you to step away from the alien.'

'Oh,' I said. 'It's you.' Because it was him. You know, the ice-cream man from the times before all this started. The one with five extra luxury flavours hidden somewhere in his van. I ignored the obvious question (i.e. what were those flavours?) and went for 'What are you doing here?' instead.

'Eeeeeeeeeee,' said Mrs Ramshaw behind me, which probably helped make up my mind a bit.

I stepped quickly away from her and then the tall ice-cream man aimed his gun at her and a frosty blue beam spat from the shooty end with a

FRAKL

and enveloped her just for a moment and then stopped.

I had so many different emotions to choose from at that moment that I had no idea whether I was going to burst into tears or kick the ice-cream man right in the 99.

'WHAT DID YOU DO THAT FOR!' I yelled. 'You said you wouldn't shoot her!'

'No, I didn't,' said the tall ice-cream man. 'Did I?'

'You sort of implied it, Terry,' said the shorter ice-cream man. The shorter ice-cream man had a nest of frizzy red hair under her cap – oh yes, and she was a woman.

'I was clearly pointing my gun at the alien. Why wouldn't I shoot it?'

'What have you done to Mrs Ramshaw?' I said.

'She's frozen,' said Terry. 'So you might as well . . .' And he smiled and waggled his eyebrows and I recognised the signs of a terrible joke about to arrive.

'If you say "Let it go" one more time, Terry, I swear by all that's holy . . .' said the redhead.

Terry rolled his eyes at me and shook his head a little.

'What have we said about not using our real names when we're on a mission, *Marjorie*,' he sighed. 'We use our code names, like the Avengers do. I'm Captain Chill,' he said to me.

Now it was Marjorie's turn to roll her eyes and

shake her head a little.

'And this is Fudge Sundae,' he said.

'I'm flippin' Marjorie, *Terry*,' said Fudge Sundae. 'I feel proper daft when you call me that.'

'I'm Leeza,' I said. 'And I get all your names but who actually *are* you if you don't mind me asking, and why are you here?'

'We're ice-cream men,' said Captain Chill, 'and we came here to use our superior technology and weaponry to kick alien butt, am I right?' And he held up his hand for a high-five from Marjorie, a high-five that Marjorie clearly had no intention of giving him.

'So you're not here to sell ice cream then?' I said as he slowly lowered his hand.

'Listen, we are this country's best and only defence against alien invasion. We roam the streets of every town in this great nation, in state-of-the-art vehicles packed to the rafters with high-tech weaponry such as this, the Big Blue Frozzypopper, and when aliens strike we are ready to drive them back where they came

115

from or, when that's not possible, contain the threat so it cannot spread!' said Captain Chill.

'Although would you like an ice cream?' said Fudge Sundae. 'Because we also sell ice creams.'

'She doesn't want an ice cream,' said Captain Chill, one hundred per cent wrongly. 'Now, we've got a job to do. Tell me, have you seen any of the big ones?'

Big ones?

'Big ones?' I said. 'Like, this big?' And I held my hands around ten centimetres apart. 'Cos I've seen a few of those.'

'Haha, no, those are the Floomins. They're the ones that get in your head. The big ones are . . .' and he held his hand way above his head, 'around this big. Oooki-Flooms, they call themselves. They're the ones in charge. They are very dangerous, so steer clear. Now, where are all your friends, the other girls and boys who go to this school?'

'They're in the hall . . . Can you help them? I think they all have Floomins in their heads.'

'Shame. Ah well. We'll just have to freeze them all,' said Captain Chill, and he pressed a button on his gun that made coloured lights switch on and off up and down its length as it made a high-pitched whine.

'You're going to . . . what?'

'Freeze the infected with the Big Blue Frozzypopper,' smiled the Captain. 'It's the only way.'

I was a bit sick of hearing about what people thought was 'the only way' this morning. Because if there's one thing I knew it's that there is always another way. And often *another* other way. That's what makes life so complicated! I looked at the door of the classroom, looked at the key still in the keyhole and made a decision.

I could see how proud Captain Chill was of his big gun.

'How does the big gun work?' I asked him, and as he proudly explained the technical gubbins I backed away till I could open the door, grabbing the key as I went, and I stepped into the corridor, slamming and locking the door as quickly as I could.

Now what?

'Run,' said Charlotte, who was running past me in the corridor.

I wasn't really in the mood for doing what I was told at this point, but she was running towards the hall, where Ishy was, and away from a group of five smiling, yellow-clad teachers who were walking amiably but with purpose towards us.

So I thought *OK then.*

And I ran.

Chapter 15

HEROES

We ran along the corridor.

'Your nose is glowing,' said Charlotte.

'Yes, yes I know,' I said. Of *course*, with all the mayhem around us, of *course* all Charlotte wanted to talk about was my nose. That was whatever the opposite of unprecedented was. It was totally precedented.

I blushed, which could only have made things worse.

That feeling was magnified by running next to Charlotte, who was like a perfectly machined tool made for dealing with situations.

I fumbled in my pocket for the battery pack that had the off switch on it. I remembered again I had an alien in my bag. *I should probably tell Charlotte*, I thought. She'd probably know why I'd done that. And then I thought I should probably tell her about the ice-cream men – that seemed like important information too.

'OK, shush,' said Charlotte. I HADN'T EVEN SAID ANYTHING.

I realised we had reached the hall doors. My mind had been all over the place, thinking about ice-cream men and Charlotte and my glowing red nose and the pickle jar, and I'd forgotten to make a plan for what to do once we got there. Get Ishy. That was it.

It would just have to do.

The hall was still full of children but now they were evenly spaced in rows, facing away from us, looking at the stage where Miss Duffield was addressing them.

Miss Duffield, in normal times, had the general air of a lady so allergic to children that if one got within two metres of her she might actually burst into flames, and she moved and acted accordingly. 'Timid' is one way of putting it. 'Trepidatious' is another, but it's very hard to spell so we'll stick with timid.

And there she was, happy and erect, eyes *not* nervously flicking from side to side, chin *not* trembling like she was one cheeky question away from bursting into tears.

She was strutting back and forth on the stage, as proud as a pigeon in a pile of crisps.

'What's going on?' I whispered to Charlotte.

She didn't answer, which was probably the right thing to do in this circumstance, while we were spying on the enemy. She was so much better at this sort of thing than I was!

'Floomins!' said Miss Duffield in a voice that wasn't quavering and apologetic. Say what you like about this alien invasion, it was doing wonders for everyone's self-esteem.

'Yes, miss!' bellowed the massed ranks of children.

One of those children was Ishy. I hoped he had added a whispered 'take' after the 'miss' like he would have done usually but I doubted it. Was that an improvement or not?

'We are pleased to announce that Owt School is merging with FloomCorp to officially form the Academy of Winners and Winning. The future is today! You, the Floomins, will drive that future! You, the Floomins, will drive productivity! You, the Floomins, will drive these children! YOU MAY NOW REJOICE.'

'YAY!' everyone shouted. I . . . t was the right noise, it was delivered at the right volume but . . . honestly, I couldn't detect any actual joy. It was like Mr Gofforth nodding and smiling when I didn't buy his beautiful pasty.

But if you're making the moves and the sounds of happiness, maybe that's enough?

I looked over at Charlotte. Maybe she'd know what we should do. She looked ready for anything. She was crouching, poised. Her piercing blue eyes, alert. Her fists balled in readiness, bloody.

How did she get bloody knuckles?

Miss Duffield was talking again.

'There will now be a short break while we prepare the pumps . . . um . . . classrooms. Please remain parked until then.'

And she strode off the stage with a swagger, like a little dog who'd found the world's biggest stick.

Now was the time to rescue Ishy. I looked at Charlotte expectantly.

'What do we do now?' I said, hoping she would say, 'We rescue Ishy, of course,' and that we would then rescue Ishy together.

'Miss Duffield teaches history,' she said, which was true but maybe not that relevant to rescuing Ishy. 'I need to knock that thing out of her head.'

OK, she knew that punching them got results. Oh heck, that might explain her bloody knuckles. What had she been doing while I had been busy running away from various people and things? Hero stuff, I supposed. But then she must also know that violence is only a temporary fix.

I was about to say, 'That's only a temporary fix,' just in case she *didn't* know but she was off, sprinting into the hall, past the parked kids, on to the stage and out the back.

Everyone in this school had their own personal mission. And it all seemed crazy! All I wanted to do was rescue Ishy and then go and get some proper help. The police, maybe. Or the army. Or, heck, I'd settle for the Girl Guides or the Pottery Club at this point. Just not . . .

FRAKL

The floor beneath my feet turned sparkly and blue and my feet slipped and slid a little.

Great. The ice-cream men were free.

'OK, FREEZE!' shouted Captain Chill, and that line wasn't getting any funnier.

'I am. I am,' I said. I put my hands up as Captain Chill and Fudge Sundae tramped down the corridor towards me.

'I was just going to go in there and rescue my friend, if that's OK,' I said.

'No, I'm afraid that's not possible. No, if your friend is in there she's infected, and that's that. No, I'm afraid we'll have to freeze her with the others.'

'But you can un-infect them,' I said. 'I knocked Mrs Ramshaw to the ground in room 2c and the thing came out of her head. And you can capture them once they're out. I've got one in a pickle jar.'

I didn't really think violence was the answer but at least it was the start of an idea.

'Oh, did you now? And how many infected do you think there are in this school, young lady? Do we need a pickle jar for each of them? Oh, I'll just go and buy three hundred pickle jars, will I? Do you know how much that would cost? We're not made of money, you know. Please, just move out of the way of the doors and let us do our job. The sooner we start, the sooner it will be finished.'

I couldn't argue with that, mostly because it was such a stupid, obvious-yet-pointless thing to say.

I really, really needed to rescue Ishy.

'Tell you what, young lady, you wait here and Fudge Sundae will get you an ice cream, how about that? And a badge. Would you like a badge? Young ladies like badges, don't they?'

He was talking to me like a . . . like I was some sort of *young lady* when in fact I was a twelve-year-old girl. It was clear he didn't realise quite what he was dealing with. I'm relatively harmless, generally, but some of us are dangerous, as he was literally seconds away from finding out.

'Aaaaaaaagh!' The scream was coming from Miss Duffield, who was pelting through the rows of children, a look of sheer terror on her face.

I had a feeling I knew what was chasing her.

'Do you have two badges?' I asked Captain Chill, 'because there's another *young lady* on her way and I'm sure she'll appreciate your offer exactly as much as I did.'

Chapter 16

HAPPY TOGETHER

Miss Duffield was nearly at the main hall doors when Charlotte Actually appeared, leaping like a hungry cheetah on to the stage. She sproinged into the rows of children, who swayed back and forth like corn in a stiff breeze as she bounded through them. Was she on all fours? She looked beautiful and terrible, like a terribly beautiful . . . *thing*. I don't know. Definitely the sort of thing that you wouldn't want chasing you.

I took two or three quick steps away from the

doors, which burst open with a BAD-DAMM, and Miss Duffield stood in the doorway, huffing and puffing, red-faced and red-eyed. 'Help me,' she whispered.

That's when Captain Chill shot her with a **FRAKL** and she toppled, blue and sparkling, to the floor with a sound like a brick hitting another brick.

'Why did you do that?' I yelled.

'It's my job!' he yelled back.

'Another target incoming!' yelled Fudge Sundae.

'Kiai!' yelled Charlotte, who had managed to cross the distance to the door in pretty much no seconds flat. She stood over Miss Duffield and I have never seen anything so heroic in my life. She had one fist clenched really tight, and with her other hand she pointed right at the ice-cream men.

'You,' she said. 'Who are you and what did you do to my teacher?'

'Charlotte, look out, they've got a freeze gun!'

I said. 'Oh, and they are ice-cream men and they—'

But Charlotte was in no mood for explanations. 'Miss Duffield is supposed to be teaching history right now. How can she teach me history if she's frozen like this? How do I unfreeze her?' she said.

'I do not have time for this,' said Captain Chill. 'Calm down or I'll have to, er . . .' And he aimed his gun at Charlotte, which struck me as a very foolish thing to do. It also struck me that maybe now was the time to rescue Ishy, while all this drama was going on.

I heard Charlotte growl as I slipped stealthily through the doors and into the hall, quietly closing the doors behind me.

I dashed through the rows of silent, motionless children, looking desperately till I found Ishy, also still, also silent, smiling like he'd never been happier.

I did not like it one little bit.

I needed to rescue Ishy from what looked like

blissful happiness, and there was only one way I knew how to do it. I had to hit him, hard. Hopefully that would knock the jelly man out of his head and then we'd just have to run far, far away from all this. We'd blow this joint and get some proper grown-up help.

I know it doesn't sound very heroic but, from the sounds of banging, shooting and shouting I could hear in the corridor outside, the actual 'heroes' were busy fighting each other and I was all that was left.

I clenched my fist and raised it. I looked at it. It looked weird.

I had never hit anyone, not properly. Not in anger. It's just not something I'd ever done.

I stepped up to Ishy. *Here we go then*, I thought.

I leaned in and whispered in his ear, 'I'm sorry about this but I'm going to have to give you a proper slap in the chops because, er . . .' I looked around but nobody was taking a blind bit of notice. OK, I could say this. 'I need you.

I can't do this without you.'

Even though nobody would be listening to this beautiful, heartfelt and potentially awkward moment I had dropped my voice and moved my head even closer to his.

There was a hint of red on his cheeks. Was he blushing?

Bless the big goof, he was embarrassed!

He wasn't massively into public shows of affection. He was the very opposite of a hugger. I'd tried hugging him a couple of times early in our friendship and it was like trying to hug a stepladder; he would go as stiff as a board.

'Durrrrr,' he said.

I was so shocked I stepped back, knocking into a parked kid in the row behind me.

Ishy's face stopped glowing red. He was silent again.

What?

I stepped up to him and his face glowed red again.

'Durrr. Durrr. Do you reck reck reck,' he said.

I stepped back again. The red glow left his face again. Silent again. Oh. Wait.

He wasn't embarrassed. The red had come from the glow of my schnozzdongle. I was bathing Ishy's face in infrared light beamed from my nose and it seemed to be doing something.

I pulled the prongs of my dongle out of my nostrils and pushed them into Ishy's, which was VERY UNHYGIENIC but this was an unprecedented situation, which hopefully excuses me.

'DO YOU RECKON WOOWOOWOOOOOO,' said Ishy, and his whole body started juddering. The schnozzdongle shot out of his nose as a green bubble expanded from his left nostril. I instinctively stepped back, jostling the row of kids behind me again, as a gloopy Floomin dropped from Ishy's nose.

I shrieked and kicked it as hard as I could, sending it flying across the hall. It landed with a sticky splat at the feet of some random classroom-filler.

Ishy's eyes flickered, then rolled round and round like a fidget spinner in 2017.

'Do you reck...' he said. 'Do you... errrrrrrrrrrrrrrrrrrrrr...'

He was coming back to me!

'Wow!' he shouted, and he took a faltering step towards me. 'Whoa, what the hecky slam is happening?'

I was so relieved so have my Ishy back that my answer came out in a jumble.

'There's ice-cream men and aliens and weird jelly in everyone's head and I think I need a hug and I have one in my bag with the pickled onions and it keeps moving,' I said. 'I'm so glad I didn't have to punch you,' I added.

'What?' said Ishy. He looked startled. 'No hugging! You know the rules...'

'Are you OK?' I said.

'Um, no, not really,' he said. 'I'm proper freaked out, a bit scared, quite angry, um... all the emotions really.'

And I hugged him; to heck with the rules. He

went so rigid it was like hugging a school chair. It was perfect.

'You get a day pass on the hugs,' said Ishy, 'but only because you saved me from whatever's happening here. Let's not make a habit of it.'

'We need to get out of here,' I said. 'Now we have a weapon,' I held up the dongle, 'hopefully we can just leave.'

Annoyingly, Ishy didn't seem to be looking or listening to me, which was typical. He was so easily distracted even in the middle of a crisis. He was looking at something behind me.

'Leeza,' he said, and there was something about his tone of voice that worried me. 'These dongles, do they just come in the one size?'

'Yes, I think so,' I said. 'Why?'

'Look,' said Ishy, nodding his head towards the stage, where a jelly the size of an elephant had somehow appeared without us noticing.

'We're gonna need a bigger schnozzdongle,' said Ishy.

Chapter 17

SCHOOL'S OUT

The jelly on the stage was like a colossal green, translucent, partially deflated beach ball, or a lime jelly made in a mould the size of a shed.

'I don't think I'm ready, for this jelly,' Ishy half sang, like an idiot.

'We have to go – now,' I said.

The jelly on the stage quivered slightly. Was it moving slowly towards us? It was hard to tell. It had no legs, or arms, or anything, it was just a big see-through glob of wobbly danger.

Ishy said, 'I think we have time to rescue

some more.' And he grabbed my schnozzdongle off me and stuck it up G-Dog's nose with a 'Dongle upside your head. I said, dongle upside your head!'

'No!' I hissed, jumping to my feet. 'Not him!'

A gummy blob oozed and dropped out of G-Dog's nostril and Ishy kicked it across the hall before it even landed, with a shout of 'HAVE IT!'

'Wuh wuh wuh. Woooowooooowooooo! Weee waaaa woooo where are we going?' said G-Dog, rubbing his head and looking confused. This wasn't an unusual look for G-Dog, to be fair.

'Out. We're going out,' I said. I was keeping half an eye on the big jelly on the stage. A large opening the size of a manhole cover had appeared in the front of its head, like a – well, maybe it was a mouth. It was hard to tell, really.

'On a school day? All right!' said G-Dog. 'G-DOG ON TOUR!' he added unhelpfully.

Nothing about the situation seemed to be bothering him. The big jelly's front-hole quivered and . . .

'YOOOOOOM!' it bellowed.

'WHAT THE HECK IS THAT?' shrieked G-Dog, finally on the same page as the rest of us.

'YOOOOOOOM,' bellowed the wobbly colossus once more. **'Yoooom arr not ready for schooo!!'** it said, and a green, translucent tentacle-like thing the width of a car exhaust emerged from the quivering mass of its body and pointed at us.

Ishy leaned over to me and whispered, 'Do you think it's talking to us?'

And then **PLOOP PLOOP PLOOP PLOOP PLOOP**

It shot five little jelly men out from the extended tentacle, which now looked more like a tube. The snotty little goobers arced through the air, each one landing on the polished floorboards with a **PLOOT.**

'I *AM* READY FOR SCHOOL,' came a voice at the back of the hall. It was Charlotte Actually, looking a little rumpled, shirt untucked, a couple of little tears in her trouser leg. She was gripping the gun that Captain Chill had been holding earlier. 'And this ISN'T school, any more. It's some sort of factory, a machine for making children useful, and that WILL NOT DO.'

'We should go,' I said. 'Like, now.'

'Why?' said Ishy. 'I think she's going to rescue us.'

'I don't think she is,' I said. 'I don't exactly know what she wants ... I think she wants to do history.'

'I WILL NEVER BE USEFUL! G-DOG IN THE HIZZOUSE!' shouted G-Dog a little unnecessarily.

'SOMEONE is going to teach me about the Industrial Revolution or so help me I will popsicle every last one of you,' said Charlotte.

FRAKL FRAKL FRAKL FRAKL FRAKL

She effortlessly picked off the five new jellies, turning them into quite tasty-looking novelty lollies.

I was idly thinking that if the aliens had arrived looking like that, maybe on sticks, I might have voluntarily stuck one into my head, when I heard chimes from outside. The melancholy, oddly creepy tones of an ice-cream van. This did not bode well.

'Seriously, Ishy, let's go. Now, while Charlotte is distracting that big jelly. Look, the fire doors, I think we can get out there, get some help. We can't do this alone.'

'What's that sound?' said Ishy. 'Is that an ice-cream van? Can we get an ice cream on the way?'

'It's the ice-cream men but they're not here to sell ice cream. From what I can tell they're here to make things worse.'

'I cannot imagine a single situation that could be made worse by an ice-cream van,' said Ishy, just as an ice-cream van drove right into the fire doors from outside, simultaneously opening them and blocking our only exit, which was quite a feat.

'See?' I said to Ishy.

'Fair play. Although there've been assemblies

where I dreamed of something like this happening.'

I wanted nothing to do with the ice-cream men, but where the heck did they get off ramming a hall full of children with an ice-cream van?

I ran over to it through the rows of parked kids, shouting, 'This place is full of children! Get that thing out of . . . um . . .'

Yes, the last word was going to be 'here' but I was briefly distracted by the driver of the van. He was handsome and blond, and he looked mortified by what he'd just done, which I found to be refreshing. So far today the ice-cream men had either ignored me or shot at me. This one seemed different.

He put the van in reverse and backed slowly out of the hall, all the while mouthing 'Sorry' at me and doing that funny little cringey grin that emojis sometimes do.

'Ishy, over here now!' I shouted.

The fire door was unblocked, the big jelly was

currently busy firing more little jellies at Charlotte, who was currently busy shooting those little jellies with her freeze gun; there was nothing more I could do but run away and get help and take Ishy with me.

Ishy jogged over, then turned and shouted, 'G-Dog!' He turned back to me and said, 'We can't leave him behind', one hundred per cent wrongly as far as I was concerned. But I couldn't stop him, and me and Ishy and G-Dog ran out of the hole in the school and past the ice-cream van and past the temporary classrooms and over the playground and out of the gate and . . .

'Wait. Did you see that?' I hissed at Ishy.

'Um, I saw something, for sure . . . We should go and . . .'

So we went back through the playground and back to the temporary classrooms because something very strange was occurring in temporary classroom 3.

FLOOMCORP™ *WE BELIEVE THAT CHILDREN ARE THE WORKFORCE OF THE FUTURE.*

AND THE FUTURE IS NOW!

(from FloomCorp motivational poster)

Chapter 18

ROCKET FUEL

There was a steady THUMP THUMP THUMP coming from the classroom.

We peered through the window. There were fifteen kids in there, jumping. And oh my, they looked so happy doing it.

They were jumping really high. Higher than kids would normally be able to jump. They were jumping higher than even Charlotte Actually could jump, and she was the high-jump champion of our school.

And as they jumped they sang;

Up! Up! Up! We're reaching for the sky!

JUMP

The only way is up! Our eye is on the prize!

JUMP

We're all so very keen

JUMP

Like cogs in a machine

JUMP

Jumping jumping jumping as production's maximised!

JUMP

We watched them for a few seconds.

'Amazing, isn't it?' whispered Ishy. 'I can do it too.'

'Don't,' I said, because you don't jump about when you're spying on aliens, but there was no stopping him.

And he jumped. It was a good jump, but nowhere near as high as the kids in temporary classroom 3.

'Oh, weird,' said Ishy. 'I remember doing it in the hall earlier. I remember it feeling really good.'

'It was the jelly that did it,' said G-Dog glumly.

'The jelly man in your head. He's what made you happy. It made me happy too. Really happy. And you!' he said to Ishy, eyes reddening. 'You took him out of my head, you moron.'

'Hey!' I said. 'Ishy was just trying to help!'

'Oh, thank you, you fat, useless lump. You took away my super powers. Nice one!' said G-Dog, who was livening up at exactly the wrong time. He squared up to Ishy, who just shook his head.

'Wait,' I said, hoping to defuse the situation with some premium on-topic insights. 'So you're saying the jelly men are like . . . an upgrade? Like, a power-up in a video game?'

'Yeah, or a cheat code. They make you feel stronger,' said Ishy.

'Better,' said G-Dog, stepping away from Ishy again. 'Happier. More powerful. Like you could do anything.'

'But everyone is just jumping up and down in unison,' I said.

'Yeah, there's a voice in your head and it kind of tells you that's what you want to do, and it's true. Or it feels true,' said Ishy.

'So they make you do whatever you're told?' I said.

'Yeah, but you love it,' said Ishy. 'That's the mad part. You know it's pointless, somewhere in your head, but you love it anyway.'

'I'm going to get one back in my head and then I'm going to kick you over the school,' said G-Dog.

'Not if someone in charge tells you not to,' I said.

'Yeah, well,' said G-Dog, and that was all he had to say about that.

'I don't get it though,' I said. 'Like you said, Ishy, it *is* pointless. Why are the aliens doing this?'

'Maybe they just want everything to be better!' said G-Dog. 'Maybe they just want everyone to be happy. Did you stop to think about that? Maybe the aliens *should* be in charge.'

'Yeah, maybe,' said Ishy. 'But in my experience you don't get owt for nowt. There's a price to be paid for everything.'

I noticed one of the kids in temporary classroom 3 had stopped jumping. He was smiling, and puffing and panting with the exertion of the jumps.

Above his head, a metal tube was snaking from the ceiling. At the business end of the tube was what looked like a domed funnel. A funnel just the right size to . . .

FLOOTCH

We could hear it through the window, the sound of the metal dome fitting snugly on the boy's head.

The snakey metal hose twitched and pulsed with a sucking noise, like when the last bit of milkshake rattles up a straw.

'They're sucking something out of him,' I said.

'See,' said Ishy. 'Oh, they're dishing out the big smiles and super-jumping powers, but they are taking something from us.'

'They can take what they want,' shrugged G-Dog. 'It's not hurting anybody. They're probably just sucking out all the sadness.'

And it was true the tubed-up kid was still smiling. Who smiles when a metal snake clamps itself to their head?

'No,' I said. 'No, this is all kinds of wrong. I don't care how hard that kid is smiling, that's not real happiness.'

'It *felt* real,' said G-Dog. 'It felt good. It felt better than how I *was* feeling, and how I'm feeling now,' he added, and I felt something then, a pang of sympathy for the big, daft brute.

'This needs stopping,' I said. Things were bad. Really bad. I shivered. Was it my imagination or did the sky darken and the air grow colder?

No, it wasn't my imagination. Something was blocking the sun.

We looked up to see two spaceships above our school, one going up and one coming down.

They were dirty, ugly, misshapen vehicles. Mostly green but mottled with dark-orange rust patches. They were fooshing purple clouds of vaporous gas from various pipes, vents and grilles that appeared to have been stuck randomly across their bodywork in a successful effort to make an ugly thing look worse.

And each one had the words 'Another FloomCorp Looorry!' emblazoned across its side in big, blocky, sickly-yellow lettering.

Each one was dangling a large silver canister about the size of a soft drinks vending machine from its undercarriage, attached by a long silver cable with a grabby claw on the end.

The descending ship's canister landed on the roof with a mournful clong, and the claw released it.

FOOOSH

went the spaceship, and it landed beside the canister.

'Bringing back the empties,' said Ishy.

'To refill with whatever the aliens are taking from us,' I said. 'I saw those canisters in the loft. They were marked "Happinish", whatever that is.'

'Sounds like happiness,' said Ishy.

'Mmm, like a big smile looks like happiness,'

I said. 'Someone, somewhere is using these kids like we use cows and someone needs to stop it.' I looked at Ishy, and I looked at G-Dog and I added, 'And we are absolutely not the people to do it. Come on, we need to find help.'

Chapter 19

GHOST TOWN

Owt was empty.

This was weird. The streets were empty. The shops were shut, and empty. The police station was closed, and empty. All I wanted to do was to find a grown-up to help us and there was no one to be found.

'I bet if we sneaked out of school when there wasn't an alien invasion happening we'd be surrounded by grown-ups in, like, two seconds flat,' said Ishy. 'Typical, innit?'

I wasn't sure that 'typical' was the right word.

I needed to think: where was everybody?

G-Dog chose that moment to start noisily and wetly beatboxing with his stupid mouth.

'Bum-buppa-dish-bippa-bum-buppa-dish.' It was probably the most intelligent thing he'd said all day but it was still really annoying.

'WILL YOU SHUT UP!' I said.

'Why did you ask me to come if you're just going to shout at me?' he said.

'I DIDN'T ASK YOU TO COME. I DIDN'T WANT YOU TO COME, BECAUSE YOU'RE USELESS,' I shouted, and immediately regretted it.

'I didn't mean that,' I said. 'I . . . Oh, wait one . . . AH . . . AH . . . AAAAAATCHOOOOO.'

'Why'd you say it then?'

It was a good question. And I knew the answer. I said it because I wanted G-Dog to feel bad. I wanted him to be hurt. And I wanted him to be hurt so that I could feel better. For some reason I didn't want to say that out loud.

So I ignored him and fished my schnozzdongle out of my pocket, because I could feel another massive sneeze coming.

'Stop fiddling with that stupid thing and answer me,' said G-Dog. 'Why'd you call me useless? Eh? Gimme that!'

And he snatched my schnozzdongle out of my hand.

I could barely see him my eyes had watered up so bad.

AAAATCHOO ATCHOOOO
            WAH-HA-CHOOOOOO!

And that seemed to be the end of that so I wiped my eyes and got ready to get proper furious with G-Dog but before I could, he held his hand out, offering me the schnozzdongle back and I thought, *Aw, he's not so bad, he wants to help stop me sneezing*, and I reached for the dongle and it felt wrong in my hand because . . .

'YOU BROKE IT. YOU BROKE THE SCHNOZZDONGLE!'

'I didn't mean to, did I?' said G-Dog, and he sounded so pitiful I almost felt sorry for him.

'This was our only weapon against the aliens!' said Ishy.

'Fine, gosh! I'm sorry! All right?' he said, not sounding sorry at all.

I opened my mouth to have another shout but then . . . I had a choice here. I could keep the argument going. It would be easy. All I would have to do is just shout at G-Dog a bit more, call him a couple of names.

Or . . .

'Apology accepted, thank you, G-Dog.' I said it like I meant it, even though I wasn't sure I did mean it, and I smiled.

'Right, well,' said G-Dog. 'I *am* sorry. It just came apart when I dropped it when you sneezed so . . . I'm sorry.'

'It's fine,' I said. 'I mean, it's not ideal but here we are. Look at us! If you had to choose three people to fight off an alien invasion we would be right at the bottom of the list.'

Ishy laughed. 'Gosh yeah, we are the absolute worst choice!'

'So let's work together and find someone who can fight these aliens,' I said.

'Yeah, let's,' said G-Dog.

'OK, cool,' I said. 'Listen, when I was running to school I saw they were building something up by the swingy park. It said something about FloomCorp and that word is on all the posters at school so . . . maybe we should go look there?'

Nobody had any better ideas so we ran up Spiffy Bindle via Fumbleby Wend and we were just within sight of the swingy park when we stopped.

So *this* was where everybody was.

The park was packed.

It felt like the whole town was there. And in the old days, like, *yesterday*, it would have been an AMAZING sight: grown-ups kicking their legs madly on the swings, spinning aimlessly on the roundabout, laughing and joking and hanging upside down on the monkey bars. That would have been something to see.

But not today. I mean, don't get me wrong, everyone seemed to be enjoying themselves. Or at least, they were all smiling. The exact same broad, blissful smile that was trespassing on the faces of the kids at school, but they weren't on the swings or the roundabout because the swings and the roundabout had been removed. There was just a large, circular track, and half the grown-ups of the town were running round and round and round, and the other half were standing by the track looking at their wrists. They were all dressed head to toe in yellow tracksuits.

'What the absolute heck is going on here?' said Ishy.

We took a few tentative steps closer.

'I don't know, but I have a feeling they are not going to be much help to us.'

On an unseen signal everyone who was running stopped and moved to the side of the track. Each one high-fived a wrist-watcher, and then the wrist-watchers hopped on to the track and started running.

'They're just running and timing each other,' I said. 'Oh no, oh no no no,' I added, because I had just spotted my dad, running like a pro, red-faced and sweaty and smiling so wide the top of his head looked in danger of falling off. And there was Mum, also smiling, timing him.

They looked so happy. And healthy. Oh heck. This was terrible.

'I think I'm going to have to punch my parents,' I said, sinking shaky-legged to the ground.

'What?' said Ishy.

'I'll hold them down while you do it, if you like,' said G-Dog.

'Shut up, G-Dog,' said Ishy, then: 'Oh wow, Dad?' And sure enough there was Mr Ahmed jogging, straight-backed, high-kneed and happy.

'We can't punch everyone on this track,' said Ishy.

'We could try,' said G-Dog but I think that was just to be annoying, not an actual suggestion, so I ignored him.

I was sitting on the pavement, head in hands. This was all too much. What were we supposed to do? All the people who were supposed to help us, and protect us, and fight aliens for us when aliens needed to be fought, they were all busy improving their personal bests.

And my parents. What had happened to my parents? I wanted them back. I wanted my embarrassing, argumentative, farty mum and dad back.

But they were gone. Driven away.

I felt sad and weird, and a sad, weird soundtrack only helped to make me feel sadder and weirder.

TINK-TINKLE-TONK-TUNKLE-TINKLE-KLONK

The sound of slow, slightly out-of-tune chimes playing 'Teddy Bear's Picnic' echoed down the streets of Owt. It was an ice-cream van and it was the only thing moving in Owt not wearing a yellow tracksuit. Apart from me.

I stood up.

'We need to get to that ice-cream van. Maybe whoever is driving can give us a lift to the next town and then . . . something. Help will come. We can still get help. Does that sound like a plan?'

'You tell us,' said Ishy. 'You're the leader.'

Oh no, that was the last thing I wanted. I couldn't be leader; I was no good at making decisions.

'I'm not the leader, OK? I want to make that quite clear. Are we clear?'

'Yes,' said Ishy. 'You're not the leader.'

'Good,' I said. 'Now, follow me.'

Chapter 20

ROAD TO NOWHERE

The mournful chimes of the ice-cream van led us along Woofy Wynd, round the Three Sided Square and up The Dangles. It seemed to be heading out of town, and it was getting further and further away from us.

I had a feeling it was heading for The Big Road out of Owt, so we took the short cut through Shady Byway, across the Trollbridge over Dribbly Tinkle and arrived at the sign saying 'You Are Now Leaving Owt' to find the van had got there before us. Something was very wrong. It was still. Its front end was a mess of dented metal and steaming engine parts but there were no obstacles to be seen. What had it hit?

Its chime had broken. A single wobbly note echoed up and down the road at two-second intervals.

TINK ... TINK ... TINK ...

I stepped slowly towards the van – somebody might be hurt in there.

I looked up the road. Just past the van everything looked a bit off. Greenish. Slightly distorted. Like there was an almost invisible wall standing between Owt and the rest of the world.

A trebly, distorted voice crackled from the cab: INVASION HAS REACHED ALERT LEVEL FOUR. HAPPINISH PRODUCTION HAS STARTED. TAKE NO CHANCES. ALL CITIZENS OF OWT TO BE FROZEN ON SIGHT. DO YOU COPY?

There was a brief pause.

TINK ... TINK ...

'Freezing! They're going to freeze us all? On sight!?' I exclaimed. 'Did you hear that?' I said to ...

Um . . .

Where had Ishy and G-Dog disappeared to?

'Psssst!'

I turned to see them crouching behind a bush by the side of the road, frantically gesturing for me to join them. It seemed like a good idea under the circumstances.

As I scrambled to join my friend and the other one, a dazed voice came from the front of the van.

'Um, hey, so this is Craig . . . Sorry, I mean Lemontop. I'm piloting Jimmy Gelato . . . Um, so remind me . . . which is the alert level where the force field completely cuts off the town? Is that Alert Level Four? I don't remember, because I just crashed my van into an invisible force field, cutting off this town and I'm a bit dazed, over,' said Lemontop.

The crackly voice: 'Force field? OK, we're at Alert Level Seven, we're at Alert Level Seven, everyone!'

'Cool,' said Lemontop. 'Seven is my lucky number.'

'So we're definitely going to have to freeze the whole town,' said the crackly voice. 'It's the only way to stop the invasion.'

What was the point of that?

'Er . . . what?' came Lemontop's voice. 'Ow, my head! . . . OK, I'll see if I can fix the engine. Keep talking, over.'

Lemontop jumped out of Jimmy Gelato and started clanking, clonking and jiggering with the engine of the van.

'They can't freeze the whole town!' whispered Ishy. 'What the heck sort of plan is that?'

I felt numb. We'd gone looking for help, we'd found a grown-up and they were talking about freezing us all. I didn't understand.

Who was going to save everyone now?

Oh no.

It couldn't be . . .

It couldn't be us, could it?

Because . . . because look at us!

How could we be of any use? A goofball, a brute and whatever the heck I was. A sneezer.

It was too much to think about. All I knew was we were going to have to stop the ice-cream men *and* the aliens, but maybe not in that order.

'How they gonna freeze us?' whispered G-Dog. 'Throw slushies at us? I'd like to see them try.'

'Those vans are packed full of ice-based weapons,' I whispered back. 'They have this gun, the Frozzypopper, it's what Charlotte was using in the hall – it freezes people immediately. It's . . . ISHY, WHERE ARE YOU GOING?'

That last bit was whispered slightly louder and more urgently than the rest because Ishy was creeping towards the back of the van.

The crackly-radio voice continued.

'So you know that now the Oooki-Flooms have sealed off the town it'll be around fifteen minutes or so before everyone on the outside of the force field forgets the town ever existed, over.'

'We're super-sure this is FloomCorp then, over,' said Lemontop.

'Oh yeah, this is classic,' crackled the radio.

'Take over a school, get the kiddiewinks producing Happinish, keep the olds occupied with pointless exercises . . . What tracksuits they using on this one, over?'

'Um, yellow, over.'

'OK, so that's different at least. The last town was a light-purpley colour. Pretty unfashionable. At least yellow is kind of bright, like a daffodil. I like yellow. The rest of it's textbook FloomCorp. Anyway, that's it, I'm afraid. There's nothing more we can do, over.'

'And how long did you say we had before everyone out there forgets us in Owt, over?' said Lemontop.

'Who is this, over?' crackled the radio.

'It's Lemontop, over,' said Lemontop.

'Who?' crackled the radio. 'Please get off the radio, this channel is for ice-cream men, over.'

'It's Lemontop. You were literally just talking to me, over,' said Lemontop.

'I don't know who you are or why I'm talking to you. This conversation is over, over.'

If I was reading the situation correctly, Owt was now completely cut off from the rest of the world, and the rest of the world now had no idea that Owt had ever even existed.

We were alone.

Lemontop continued to faff with his van. If anything he was ramping up the faffing, and the clanking and clonking was getting louder and louder.

Ishy had managed to sneak all the way to the back of Lemontop's van and was opening the back doors. He stuck his head in, had a look around then beckoned us over with a huge grin.

'It's amazing!' he mouthed.

We scurried over as quietly as we could. 'What? What have you found?' I whispered.

Ishy opened the back door wide.

'Ice cream!' he whispered triumphantly. 'Loads of it.'

Chapter 21

BEEN CAUGHT STEALING

I looked round the inside of the van. There was everything you were expecting from the back of an ice-cream van, unless you were expecting high-tech weaponry. Freezers full of ice cream and lollies. Shelves of boxes marked 'Wafers' and '99s'. And a big red button marked 'DO NOT PRESS', which Ishy had gravitated towards immediately and was just about to press.

'Ishy,' I hissed. 'Maybe we shouldn't—'

He pressed it. Of course he did.

WHIIIIZZZZT WOZZZZZT FUNF

The freezers and shelves spun round and

suddenly we were surrounded by big blue guns. Frozzypoppers.

'Oh yeah,' said Ishy.

'Gimme!' said G-Dog.

'What are you doing in here?' said Lemontop, who was suddenly peering in through the back of the van.

I couldn't think of anything to say. Luckily we had a goofball in the team.

Ishy smiled. 'Hey up, how's your belly for spots?' he said, which was a good response. It certainly had the element of surprise going for it.

Meanwhile G-Dog's response was to immediately grab a Frozzypopper and point it at Lemontop.

'Back off, blondie,' he said. He had a knack for finding something obvious and physical about whoever he was talking to and just saying it out loud.

'Sneezy and Biggins, get behind me,' he said.

'Oh, that's brilliant,' said Lemontop. 'That's just brilliant. After the day I've had so far? Go on, just point a gun at me, why don't you? Do you know what? I'm done with this.'

He pulled his peaked cap off his head, letting his startlingly shiny blond hair tumble delightfully to his shoulders.

'You want the gun? Here, you might as well have the hat too. Actually, you know what? Take the van. It's yours. Why not? Haha. Do what you like with it, cos in about two hours none of it's going to matter because we're all going to get frozen and do you know what? Looking at you, I'm glad.'

He threw his hat at G-Dog's face and turned and stomped off down the road towards Owt, presumably because all other directions were cut off by the force field.

'That was unexpected,' said Ishy as we watched Lemontop go. He was already wearing the hat Lemontop had thrown at us. That was Ishy in a nutshell. If there was a hat in the vicinity it would always wind up on his head before too long. It was the same impulse that would lead him to press any button marked 'Do not press'.

He pressed the DO NOT PRESS button.

WHIIIIZZZZT WOZZZZZT FUNF

All the Frozzypoppers disappeared into the walls, replaced by the packed freezer units.

'Would anyone like an ice cream?' he said. 'The Mighty Thor said it was all right.'

'Look, I think we just need a quick recap,' I said, banging the DO NOT PRESS button and

WHIIIIZZZZT WOZZZZZT FUNF

getting rid of the ice creams, which were clearly a distraction from the task at hand.

'There is an ALIEN INVASION happening out there. Our friends and our families have been taken over by actual little green men, and even though they look happy about it—'

'I've never seen my dad so happy,' said Ishy, hitting the DO NOT PRESS button.

WHIIIIZZZZT WOZZZZZT FUNF . . . ice cream.

'I didn't see mine but I'd be surprised if even

an alien pulling levers in his head could make the grumpy old git happy,' said G-Dog.

'We tried to get help, but help is all gone.' I banged the DO NOT PRESS button again.

WHIIIIZZZZT WOZZZZZT FUNF . . . guns.

'And . . . oh gosh, I can hardly believe I'm saying this, but it looks like it's up to us to save the town,' I said. 'ISHY, SO HELP ME, IF YOU HIT THAT BUTTON ONE MORE TIME I WILL SHOOT YOU MYSELF.'

'You won't,' said G-Dog. 'I've been trying to shoot him for the last two minutes but I can't get this gun to work.'

'What?' I said, and I grabbed the gun off him, pointed the shooty end at the ceiling and pulled the trigger. Nothing.

'Brilliant. We've got a broken-down van full of guns that don't work. What are we going to do?'

'Pass it here,' said Ishy. 'I'm mint at computer games, and they've all got different control systems. I reckon I could work this out no bother with a bit of time.'

'YOOOOOOOOOOOOM!'

The sound was so loud the fixtures in the van rattled, and so did my spine.

'YOOOOOOOOM MUST RETURN TO THE ACADEMY AND START ACHIEVING IMMEDIATELY IF OUR TARGETS ARE TO BE MET.'

It was the giant jelly from before.

'What's that?' squeaked G-Dog.

'It's the biggest jelly you've ever seen and it wants us to go back to school,' I said. 'What are we going to do?'

'You know what I like with my jelly?' grinned Ishy.

WHIIIIZZZZT WOZZZZZT FUNF

We were doomed.

FLOOMINS! The workforce of the future! Simply pop them into the head of any species of alien to transform those aliens into happy, productive workers. We found a whole planet of these gummy little marvels just wasting their time, dancing all day and dancing all night! FloomCorp scooped up the lot and worked out how to harness their mind-control powers! They are compact and easily stored within our own, disgustingly gelatinous bodies! They don't complain – they can't! We've brainwashed them! Hahaha!

We rule, you guys, serioooosly!

(Internal FloomCorp ooomail)

Chapter 22

HOMEWARD BOUND

We shuffled over to the serving hatch window and peered out.

There it was, more jelly than you'd need at a hundred children's birthday parties, quivering in agitation by the side of the road.

'PLEASE PREPARE TO GET READY FOR SCHOOL,' it boomed, and a gelatinous tube formed from its wobbly mass, about as wide as an exhaust pipe and . . .

PLOOP PLOOP PLOOP

Three little jelly men were pumped out, each one catching the sunlight on their shiny green bodies as they arced towards the van.

They disappeared from our view but we heard the **sPLoTCH sPLoTCH sPLoTCH** of them landing on the roof.

The tube melted away back into Big Jelly's body, leaving just a small indentation where it would emerge again.

Pitter pitter pitter

The jelly men were on the move.

'Is the back door closed properly?' I hissed, then the van dipped slightly like . . . like someone had got in, but someone bigger than a jelly man.

'Hey, kids. I just wanted to apologise for what I said earlier. I'd just had some very sad news,' came the voice of Lemontop from the front of the van. 'But I shouldn't have taken it out on you, that was wrong. Hold on. I'm going to get us out of here.'

The van lurched into life, tyres screaming, and we reversed at high speed down the road to Owt and away from the Oooki-Floom, the first note of 'Teddy Bear's Picnic' blaring loudly and eerily as we went.

TINK-TINK-TINK-TINK

'He's lying,' whispered G-Dog. 'He's taking us somewhere to freeze us.'

'How do you know he's lying?' I whispered back.

'Did you ever hear anyone apologise like that? Especially a man. What a load of baloney.'

'G-Dog might be right,' piped up Ishy. 'I'm not sure we can take the chance. I think we need to get out of here.'

'Where to?' said Lemontop. 'Aaagh, Floomins on the windscreen! One moment, hold on.' He slammed on the brakes. 'I just need to deal with these.' And he jumped out of the van with a freeze gun.

'Well, if we're going to run, now's the time,' I said. 'But he's got the van, so . . .'

'Don't worry about the van,' said G-Dog, holding up a banana. 'G-DOG!' he added, louder than necessary.

Ishy said, 'We should each take one of these.

They might come in handy.' He grabbed a Frozzypopper and handed it to me.

I pushed open the back doors and we ran for it, pausing for G-Dog to stuff a banana up the van's exhaust.

'How many of those have you got?' I asked.

'A bunch,' he shrugged. 'Let's do one!'

We ran straight off the road and into the trees, heading via Hobb's Dawdle to Fairy Glen, which we could cut through to get to The Scabby Patch and then back up The Big Narrow and then . . .

'Where are we going?' said G-Dog.

'We need somewhere safe to prepare to . . . to do whatever we're going to do. We're quite close to mine, and it's empty, because my parents are . . . busy.'

And that's how we wound up at my house.

I opened the front door and I was just about to say 'Make yourself at home,' when Ishy and G-Dog pushed past me, Ishy heading for the sofa and G-Dog for the kitchen.

By the time I had closed the door I could hear

the TV was on and so, apparently, was the microwave.

Kitchen first, because goodness knows what G-Dog was up to in there.

'What are you microwaving?'

'Nothing,' said G-Dog sulkily.

Through the window of the microwave the light started sputtering and flickering. He was literally microwaving nothing, which was literally the wrongest thing you can do with a microwave.

The microwave went PHUT and that was it. A small sorry strand of smoke wound its way up to the ceiling from the top vents.

'Oh my gosh, my mum will freak when she sees this,' I said.

'Nah, she'll probably just smile,' shrugged G-Dog.

'Why are you constantly trying to start an argument, G-Dog?'

'You wanna know why?'

'Well . . . Yes, yes I do.'

'At least when you're telling me off you're talking to me.'

'Is that it? Is that why you keep breaking things and name-calling?'

He shrugged.

'OK, well.' I didn't know what to say. I wasn't expecting an emotional truth bomb from the daft lug. I sighed. 'You know what, I really did like your dancing yesterday, by the way.'

'Did you?' he said, his face brightening.

'Yes, yes I did. You really looked . . .' *like a walrus attempting ballet* . . . 'like you were enjoying yourself.'

G-Dog nodded and looked down. He was blushing.

From the living room came the sound of the latest summer pop sensation.

'ISHY!' I shouted. 'ARE YOU WORKING OUT HOW TO FIRE THAT GUN OR ARE YOU WATCHING TELLY?'

'Can't I be doing both?' shouted Ishy from the living room.

I stomped through to find him clicking through various music channels, the big blue gun resting next to him on the sofa.

'Ishy, the gun,' I said.

'In a minute,' he said. The options on screen kept refreshing as he pressed the remote, and my schoolbag started bucking and jiggling and bopping against my side.

I pulled the bag off and threw it to the ground.

It hopped about.

'Ishy,' I said.

'I will,' he said.

'No, look.'

He stopped faffing with the remote and looked where I was pointing, at my schoolbag, which was on the floor, motionless.

'It's a nice bag,' he smiled. 'Have I not said that before? I like it.'

And he went back to pressing the remote and the bag started jumping again and . . . Wait a minute.

'Ishy,' I said. 'I think—'

But my thought was interrupted, first by G-Dog, who said, 'Weird! I think the remote is controlling your bag!' and then by the **PIT! PAT! SPLOOT! PHLAT!** of hundreds of tiny jelly men hitting all the windows in our house. It was raining Floomins. Hallelujah.

Chapter 23

DRY THE RAIN

Ishy shrieked and rolled off the sofa to the floor.

G-Dog sprinted to the kitchen and ran back carrying a knife. It was a butter knife but then the Floomins looked quite spreadable so maybe that was the right idea.

I jumped the sofa, being careful not to land on Ishy, and grabbed the remote control from where he'd dropped it.

The front door started rattling. So did the windows. We were surrounded.

'Ishy, did you get the gun working?' I said.

'Nearly,' came a voice from under the sofa. His

hand appeared, patted up and down the sofa until it found the gun, then dragged it down out of sight.

I opened my bag and pulled out the jar of Floomin I'd had in there pretty much all day. I set the jar down and pointed the remote at it and started mashing buttons. Every time I jabbed a button on the remote the Floomin moved, or froze, or stretched, or jiggled. It seemed random but then I was pushing buttons randomly.

I took a risk. I unscrewed the jar and tipped the Floomin out and stepped back. It made no attempt to jump for my face. I decided to present a bigger target. I flared my nostrils, then held them open with my fingers. The Floomin twitched, then rolled slowly round in a small circle on the carpet.

OK then.

'G-Dog, take this and point it at the door,' I tossed him the remote, 'and just click it like crazy. I don't know how but it does something to the Floomins. It stops them wanting to obey orders maybe?'

'Infrared!' said Ishy from under the sofa.

'Why are you shouting colours?' said G-Dog. 'ORANGE!' he added.

'Infrared is what remote controls shoot out,' said Ishy. 'Like an invisible laser.'

'Oh wow,' said G-Dog. 'Sweet. Good knowledge!'

I didn't have time to stand and applaud this new breakthrough in Ishy/G-Dog relations. I needed more weapons. I ran up the stairs into Mum and Dad's room. It was a mess and I briefly stood and remembered a time when my parents were the messy, slobby, annoying, amazing humans they used to be. I was getting nostalgic for last Saturday afternoon! I suddenly felt quite old, and then I felt quite frightened as I was snapped out of my daydream by more little Floomins hitting the windows.

I grabbed the remote that was half sticking out from under a pair of grey underpants and ran into my room, grabbing my own remote from in there.

Downstairs I found G-Dog was saying, 'So you reckon that infrared light can transmit information in low data rates, and that's probably why Leeza's infrared dongle discombobulated the Floomins? Like, it's changed their channels or something?'

'For real,' said Ishy. 'And look, if you press "mute" it kind of switches off the Floomin altogether.'

He aimed his remote at the Floomin, clicked mute, and it fell over on to its back and lay there, its stubby little legs pointing skywards.

'You're, like, all wise like a proper Yoda with this stuff,' said G-Dog. 'Nice one. PURPLE!' he added loudly. 'Oh, I forgot we weren't just shouting colours.'

'Get to the windows and mute these monsters!' I said. 'Here, Ishy, grab this!'

I tossed him a remote and we started 'firing', mashing MUTE again and again. The little Floomins outside started dropping to the ground. It was working. I was aiming at the windows,

G-Dog was aiming at the front door and Ishy . . .

'Ishy, why are you aiming it at the telly?'

'I was going to find an appropriate playlist or something but . . . I can see by your face that you do not think that is a good use of my time. I'll go upstairs and shoot out of the windows there.'

We kept clicking and the Floomins kept dropping. From upstairs Ishy shouted, 'They just keep coming! There's one of those big jellies out there and he's shooting little ones out of that mad pipe they all have.'

I remembered that pipe from the attack on the ice-cream van. I didn't know how many little Floomins a big jelly could shoot out of itself, and I didn't really want to have to wait until it had run out.

I aimed my remote at the big jelly. I clicked and clicked the MUTE button but it had no effect. It kept on firing little gummies out of its gummy pipe. Clearly the remote was only effective against the little ones.

That pipe though, that slimy, gelatinous pipe.

It was around the size and shape of a . . .

'G-Dog, you still got any bananas?'

'Yes, why? Is it some sort of middle-class snack time I wasn't aware of?'

I explained what I wanted him to do and his face lit up.

'This is PEAK G-DOG!' he shouted, louder than necessary.

'Ishy,' I shouted up the stairs. 'G-Dog is going out there. You and me need to cover him!'

'Awesome!' shouted Ishy from upstairs. 'I've been playing first-person shooters on the consoles since before I was supposed to be allowed to. I can lay down covering fire, no problem!'

'Is everyone ready?' I asked, and nobody said yes. That seemed about right. Who could really say, hand on heart, that they were ready to stick a banana up a giant jelly monster?

'One . . . Two . . . Three!' I kicked open the front door and started clicking like crazy. G-Dog ran down the path, Floomins flying at him from all directions, almost too many of them for me and Ishy to pick off with our remotes . . .

. . . but *not* too many of them for me and Ishy to pick off with our remotes. Floomins were dropping like someone was repeatedly smashing an invisible Floomin piñata in the vicinity. I was getting a serious cramp in my thumb though as G-Dog made it to the giant jelly that was wobbling and glistening in the middle of our street.

The thing is, it was big, and it was scary, but it wasn't fast. G-Dog ran to within two metres of the creature, then stopped and turned to face the house. He smiled, then he mouthed something at us. Ah, no, he wasn't talking, he was beatboxing, and then the cocky little hooligan spun round in an approximation of some kind of dance move and . . .

FLOOOOOTCH!

He rammed the banana right into the alien's Floomin-pipe.

He spun again, then bowed, and then walked away from the beast with a swagger that was both comical and yet also oddly heroic.

The creature started to judder, and then it expanded, then contracted, again and again as it tried, presumably, to shift the banana that was causing a blockage.

'Go G-Dog,' I laughed, before adding, 'oh no, G-Dog, look out!' as the big alien shot a tentacle out of its body, a large gloopy protuberance about the width of a tree trunk, aimed right at G-Dog's happy little head.

G-Dog never knew what hit him.

Chapter 24

LIGHT AND DAY

Because nothing hit him. Just as the tentacle was about to smash into him a sparkly blue beam hit it from the side with a **FRAKL** and it went from bright green to frosty blue in an instant and clonked to the road, stiff and unmovable. Then with another **FRAKL** the rest of the beast followed suit.

Lemontop ran up the road, and in my head he was going in slow motion. Every time I remember this moment (which is often) I recall the way the sunlight danced across the gold of his hair ... and the memory is only slightly spoiled by the indelible memory of the way G-Dog's face crinkled up in actual furious disbelief, like a baby tasting a lemon for the first time, when Lemontop physically picked him up and ran with him into my house.

'You're safe now, little man,' said Lemontop as he gently placed G-Dog down on to the living-room carpet. I couldn't help it, I burst out laughing and I was only slightly ashamed when I saw the hurt reactions of both G-Dog and Lemontop.

'Little man, oh, bless the pair of you,' I said. Then 'Sorry,' because I didn't mean to embarrass them, then 'OH NO' because the pickle jar was lying empty on the carpet at G-Dog's feet, but where was the Floomin I'd caught? In all the excitement I'd forgotten to put it back in the jar! And now it was loose somewhere in the house. This was the last thing we needed.

'Ishy, are you OK?' I shouted, and Ishy came down the stairs with a 'My belly is great for spots if that's what you're asking,' so that was a relief.

He jumped the last five steps and rushed to high-five me and G-Dog.

'That was amazing!' he said. 'Did you see that? We were all like *pew pew pew* with the remotes and the aliens were like *o wow they got me* plop plop plop all falling to the ground and that was great, wasn't it?'

'Stay on your guard cos there's one loose in here,' I said. 'Thanks for saving G-Dog,' I added to Lemontop.

'Did he heck as like save me!' said G-Dog indignantly. 'I'm the one that saved everyone, I banana'd the big boss, you're all welcome.'

'No one was saved,' said Lemontop with a sigh, and that killed the mood pretty quickly. He sat on Dad's scruffy armchair with another sigh. 'I'm not sure you understand what's going on here.'

And he was right, I didn't understand. I just knew something bad was happening, and I also knew that when something bad starts happening you have to go and get help, find someone to sort it out for you, but everyone was . . . they were all . . .

I sat down on the carpet. I sighed too, because sighs are catching.

'What's going on, Lemontop?' I asked.

'Craig,' he said. 'Lemontop is my ice-cream-man name and I recently resigned.'

'Oh? Why'd you resign?' I said.

'Because what's the point of us?' he said. 'When I joined the ice-cream men I thought I'd be saving the world, fighting aliens, thwarting evil plans, selling the occasional three-scoop delight, but that's not what it's like at all. We try, we really do, but then something like this happens. The Oooki-Flooms come down, build one of their awful factories, put up a force field and because any time you get close to them they throw a little jelly man up your nose that makes you perfectly happy with what the Oooki-Flooms are doing, we can't do a thing about it. The only thing we *can* do is freeze everyone to stop the Floomins spreading. And then freeze ourselves. And I didn't know *that* until someone on the outside of the force field explained it to me, so here we are. Would you like to be frozen before I freeze myself, or what?'

'We have a weapon. We know how to stop them,' I said.

'OK?' said Lemontop, his face suddenly hopeful. 'Do you?'

'Remote controls. Somehow . . .'

'Infrared,' said Ishy. 'And while you were running round doing useful things like knocking holes in the school and freezing schoolchildren, we were kicking back and wasting time watching the telly, and guess who found the one thing that can defeat the aliens? Team Timewaster. Yeah.'

He held his hand up for a high-five, which I returned, and so did G-Dog with a slightly louder than necessary 'G-DOG WASTING TIME IN THE HOUSE!'

'OK, so how does it work?' said Lemontop.

'Dunno, really. Somehow the infrared signal messes with the little Floomins' instructions. It stops them doing what they do, or it makes them do something else. Or something,' said Ishy.

'Right. Great. How many remote controls do you have?'

'Uh, three?' I said.

'Do you know how many Floomins there are in this town?'

'Uh . . . do you?'

'Well, there's, what, six thousand people living in Owt? Which means there are at least six thousand Floomins. You'd need to get them all at once to even stand a chance. Basically you're going to need a bigger remote control.'

'What if we could control the big jellies?' said Ishy. 'Like, if we could use the remote to secretly change things in their heads?' He padded over to the window and started clicking at the big frozen beast in the road.

'I tried that, Ishy,' I said. 'The big ones don't seem to be affected.'

'It makes a pretty pattern though!' said Ishy. 'Aw, it's amazing. Look! And bring your remote.'

Going to the window to look at a pretty pattern seemed on the one hand like a total waste of time. But on the other hand it seemed like the most defiant thing we could do in a town where everyone else was working hard to achieve goodness knows what. Wasting time seemed like the most human thing we could be doing at that moment.

So we joined Ishy at the window as he pointed his remote at the frozen Oooki-Floom in the street. 'Infrared light is usually invisible, but something about the alien jelly: when it's crystallised by the Frozzypopper, it creates . . .'

'Do you have to wang on? Can't you just show us?' grumbled G-Dog.

Ishy could have bitten at that, started an argument, but he didn't, he just smiled and nodded and said, 'I am the king of wanging on,' and I was very proud of him for that.

Then he clicked, and clicked, and clicked his

remote and on the frozen surface of the big jelly the light became visible, and somehow alive. It danced, it played, it exploded like the most spectacular, soundless fireworks display you've ever seen. And it wasn't just reds; the light was refracted into a paintbox of colours.

'Each button makes a different pattern of colours,' said Ishy. 'Give it a go.'

We pointed our remotes at the icy blob and the light show intensified; beams and waves and dancing sparkles bathed the houses on both sides of the street in an ever-shifting kaleidoscope of reds, greens, yellows and every other colour you've seen, and two or three you never did unless you've ever pointed a TV remote at a frozen alien jelly.

It was beautiful and it was fun. The light played on our faces, illuminating our smiles, smiles so different to the ones stretching the faces of the Driven. Smiles of awe and wonder. It was *so* pretty and it made me feel hopeful in the way that seeing beauty in an unexpected place at an unexpected time can make you feel hope.

It was nice, but then a pretty light show never saved anyone, I thought to myself – one hundred per cent wrongly.

'That was nice. Now, teach us how to use these guns, blondie,' said G-Dog. 'It's time to get to work.'

He was wrong too.

As it turned out, a pretty light show and a feeling of hope was exactly what was going to save everybody.

But first we tried the whole 'getting to work with guns' thing. Bear with us. We'll get there.

Chapter 25

THERE'S NO OTHER WAY

'There's a secret keypad in the handle,' said Lemontop. 'Look.'

I wasn't looking at the gun, or at Lemontop, or at anything other than the frozen jelly in the road. I didn't see the point. The ice-cream men were already playing with guns and it was doing no good whatsoever. There had to be a better way. I was starting to feel like someone was going to have to take charge.

I was starting to feel like it might have to be me.

And I didn't want it to be me. It couldn't be

me, not really. I wasn't a hero. I wasn't a leader. I couldn't fire a gun or run really fast. I was just a kid with allergies in the wrong place at the wrong time, i.e. in Owt during an alien invasion. Best to keep my head down and wait for someone else to sort everything out, surely?

So I ignored the feeling and tried to distract myself by idly playing with the remote, drawing light traces across the alien, adjusting my aim so the light beams glanced at particular angles, to hit this window or that door, or make the top of a chimney or TV aerial sparkle. I was using the empty houses of my street as a blank sheet for doodling with light.

'Now, this is important. You have to aim into the main torso of whatever you want freezing. If you aim for arms or legs, your enemy will not be fully incapacitated,' said Craig. I liked him better when he was being open and honest about the way he was feeling. All this gun talk was boring and pointless as far as I was concerned.

The muted, motionless little jelly men that only ten minutes ago had been flying in the general direction of our nostrils littered the garden, the path, the road. I decided to light them up, one by one, in different colours just because I thought it might look pretty and why not?

I picked one of the colour buttons on the remote – not yellow, I was sick of yellow. I picked green – and I aimed the remote just so. Light flared from the big popsicle like a peacock's feathers and bathed our whole front path in a shimmering disco-tastic display. *Nice*, I thought. The shimmering caused the Floomins to cast long shadows, shadows that jittered and twitched and . . .

Ooops. Not good. Not good at all.

The shadows were jittering and twitching because the Floomins were jittering and twitching. They were coming back to life.

But it was OK, I still had the remote. I hit mute.

Nothing. No light. No shimmering. Floomins still moving.

Click Click Click Mute Mute Mute

Nothing.

Why would the remote have stopped working?

Oh, yeah. Why does the remote ever stop working?

'Guys, I need some batteries! GUYS! KITCHEN, MIDDLE DRAWER! Underneath a whole bunch of things that shouldn't be in that drawer!'

'Would another remote be any good?' asked Ishy.

'OF COURSE IT WOULD!' I shouted at him, snatching the remote from his hand and stuffing the broken one into my pocket. I turned to point it out of the window at the big jelly because the little jellies were . . .

Wait, what were they doing?

They weren't . . .

Were they?

Were they . . .

. . . dancing?

'Uh, guys, you might want to take a look out here.'

Ishy, G-Dog and Lemontop crowded round the window.

We watched as all the Floomins on the path stepped this way and that, then twirled, then dipped, then did a little jump and a clap then twirled again . . .

'They're dancing,' said Ishy.

'They are, aren't they?' I said.

'This is brilliant,' said G-Dog. 'Target practice!' And he stepped back, aiming his Frozzypopper out of the window.

Thankfully Lemontop snatched the gun out of his hand. I don't mean thankfully for the Floomins, I mean thankfully for G-Dog because if he'd fired that gun I think I might have actually hit him.

'The green button did it. Watch,' I said. And I aimed the remote just so, hit 'green' and bathed more of the Floomins scattered in the road in a colourful light show. They jumped up, as one, and joined in the dance.

'Look at that,' said Ishy. 'The infrared light

bouncing off that jelly, it's . . . it's refracting the light and sort of . . . remixing the Floomins. Setting them free.'

'Science with a dance beat,' said G-Dog. 'Gotta love it.'

P-TOOF – THOOMP!

That was the sound of a banana shooting out of an alien and hitting the window at high speed.

'Where did that . . . Oh no,' I said.

'YOOOOOOOOOOOM!' boomed the big jelly in the street, sending an avalanche of sparkling fragments of ice tumbling from its body. It had broken free of its icy coating.

'YOOOOOM!' it boomed again. **'CEASE THIS POINTLESS WASTE OF TIME AND ENERGY THIS INSTANT!'** And it dawned on me it was shouting at the little Floomins, not us. The Floomins stopped dancing and started cowering, some in groups of two or three, hugging each other. This big jelly was bullying the little ones.

'G-Dog, shoot it,' I said. 'Shoot it all over.'

'Gladly,' said G-Dog, taking aim.

FRAKL

'Dancing,' he said.

FRAKL

'Is not,' he said.

FRAKL

'A waste of time,' he said.

And it was the first thing he'd said all day I couldn't argue with.

'Nice grouping,' said Lemontop. I expect it was some sort of gun-jargon. Ishy and G-Dog nodded appreciatively as he added, 'Target is immobilised.'

The big jelly was fully frozen again, but surely everyone could see this was just a temporary fix.

The little Floomins outside started to dance again. But we weren't aiming light at them. They were dancing because . . . because they wanted to. And gosh, I wanted to dance too, but there were other, pressing matters to deal with.

'How long was that thing frozen for, the first time?' I asked, 'Was it, like, fifteen minutes?'

'About that, yeah,' said Lemontop. 'If the big jellies are developing immunity to the Frozzypopper then . . . I don't know, it's not good, is it?'

'We don't have long,' I said. 'These little guys aren't the enemy. Look at them. They just want to dance. All we need to do is bathe the rest of them in light reflected off a big frozen alien, which is . . .'

I looked at the big lump of ice outside.

'Which is going to be difficult but . . .'

And then I remembered the spaceships hovering over the school. The ones with the long grabby arms.

And I had an idea.

'I have an idea,' I said.

Everyone looked at me expectantly.

'What if . . . what if we go back to school and we hijack one of the spaceships that were lifting canisters up? We . . . could use it to hoist one of the big aliens into the sky and then . . . then we could use a freeze gun to freeze it and then we all aim a remote control at the frozen alien and the reflected light will bathe the whole town in all the shimmering colours and the Floomins will all be hit at once and . . . Ishy? G-Dog? What? Stop it. Stop it now.'

But they didn't hear me, they were all laughing too loudly. They were all laughing at me. Not just tittering, or chuckling, but full-on eyes-streaming, snot-flowing hilarity.

'BRILLIANT PLAN!' honked G-Dog. 'Apart from it being utterly ridiculous and totally impossible I think it's a goer! HAHAHAHA!'

'HAHAHAHAHAHAHAHAHA! Have you heard her?' said Ishy in between ugly, gasping snorts for breath. 'We're going to steal a spaceship, lads. Heck, let's steal two while we're at it! Oh, Leeza, that's brilliant.'

My eyes were prickling. My cheeks were flushing. I am allergic to a lot of things but embarrassment is the worst and it can't be cured even by sticking a remote control up your nose and clicking 'mute'. I know because I tried. So I ran upstairs and locked myself in my bedroom instead.

Chapter 26

ALONE AGAIN OR

I huddled in the corner of my room with my legs drawn up to my chest and I stared at the wall.

'Leeza.' Ishy's voice came through my door. 'We're sorry, please come out.'

The thing is, they were right, my plan was hopeless and pointless. This is why I don't like making decisions, or plans, or making suggestions for interesting things to do. You have an idea and it's terrible and it's embarrassing and awful. How could I have possibly thought that we could foil an alien invasion?

'Gerroff me!' said Ishy.

'You need to bang the door harder!' said G-Dog.

THUMP THUMP THUMP

'Come on, open the door! Just because your idea was really stupid, it—'

'G-Dog, really?' said Ishy.

'I'm sorry! I didn't mean stupid! I meant . . .' G-Dog lowered his voice. 'Ishy, you know words and stuff. What's a nicer word for stupid?'

The door rattled and banged.

OK. So my plan was an absolute pointless waste of time. But it was my time to waste. And what if I wanted to waste it trying to make things better rather than waiting to be put on ice?

Maybe it would be better if I just found a Floomin and stuffed it up my nose. Maybe I would be happier if I was happy all the time. Maybe just jumping up and down was exactly what I needed.

Why did allowing myself to be very happy indeed, for ever, seem like a defeat?

THUMP THUMP THUMP

Pitter pitter pitter

What was that sound?

Oh, Leeza! Be careful what you wish for!

Pitter pitter pitter

My blood ran as cold as ice cream. It was the escaped Floomin. It was in the room with me. I could hear it but I couldn't see it.

Pitter pitter pitter

Did I just see the duvet move?

'Help!' I shouted, just as the door went THUMPTHUMPTHUMP again so no one could hear me, and then I saw the Floomin and it was right in front of me, standing still on the carpet and it was holding batteries.

Why was it holding batteries?

It was holding two AA batteries, grasping them between its two green stubby arm-things. It dropped them to the carpet and gave them a nudge towards me and then it stepped back.

No way! It was trying to help me. And it had listened to me. It knew the batteries were in the middle drawer in the kitchen underneath all the stuff that shouldn't be in that drawer.

'Thank you,' I said. 'Thank you . . .'

What was its name? It had come from a pickle jar, so . . .

'Thank you, Pickle,' I said.

I pulled my remote from my back pocket, emptied the old batteries and reloaded.

The Floomin flung its arms and head back, standing with its legs spreadeagled, like it was waiting for something.

'What do you want?' I said. 'Do you want . . . ?' And I waggled the remote.

It threw its stubby little arms even further back, and I took that as a 'yes'.

I aimed. Pressed 'green'. The Floomin juddered briefly then its foot tapped. Its head nodded. Its leg moved back and forth. And then it started dancing to the rhythm of G-Dog banging on my door and I made up my mind right there.

And maybe I climbed straight out of the window, or maybe I wasted two minutes dancing with the Floomin first. Either way, five minutes later I was stepping carefully around the dancing Floomins in the road outside my house. They moved and grooved and seemed oblivious to me. They seemed happy. Really genuinely happy, as far as you can tell when a blob of jiggling jelly is happy. I cautiously tiptoed past the big frozen jelly in their midst, then hurried along Bushy Waffles, taking the secret short cut through The Duck Woof, over Grassy Tum until, finally, I was outside the school.

There was no one else outside. Whatever was happening to my classmates was happening behind closed doors. I could see an ugly green spaceship still parked on top of the roof.

Right, then. The plan was on.

I breathed deeply. OK, I knew that what I was about to try was probably never going to work. But someone had to do something, and I was the only one willing to do it.

I didn't have a choice.

'Up up up, we're reaching for the sky!'

Oh no. I whirled round – the singing had

come from behind me. It was Ishy, and G-Dog, and Lemontop. They stood motionless, smiling. Smiling really wide.

Oh no. Oh no no no. I never should have left them! They'd been infected.

Ishy trembled, then shook, then . . .

'Bahahahaha!' laughed Ishy. 'You should see your face!'

'Hooohohoho! Oh, that was good!' laughed G-Dog.

'Actually, I think it was pretty cruel,' said Lemontop. 'Funny, but cruel.'

'You IDIOTS!' I shouted. 'I am so glad to see you. Thank you. Thank you!'

'We couldn't let you do this alone,' said Ishy.

'Or fail to do it alone,' said G-Dog.

'And we had nothing better to do,' said Ishy.

'And I feel partially responsible for this mess, being an ice-cream man and everything,' said Lemontop.

'So hey! Do you reckon we could foil an alien invasion, just the eighty of us?' said Ishy.

'What? *How* many?' I said.

'Look behind us,' said Ishy.

Oh. Wow. Eighty little blobs of jelly had trotted up behind my friends.

'They led us here,' said Ishy. 'I think they want to help.'

Were they looking at me? It was hard to tell. I waved and eighty stubby little arms waved back.

'Gosh, OK. To answer your question, Ishy,' I said, eyes prickling again, maybe because of pollen, maybe not. 'Yes. Yes, I do think we can foil an alien invasion with just the eighty of us. Cos there were just three of us to start with, weren't there? And then four,' I nodded at Lemontop, 'and now there's loads. Who knows how many more of us there'll be by the time we finish. So. Yes. I do reckon. I really do.'

'There was just one of us first,' said Ishy. 'Before there were three, there was just you.'

'Can I just say . . .' said G-Dog, and I really wanted to stop him because he had a knack of saying the wrong thing at the wrong time but I didn't have the energy to stop him so . . .

'Can I just say I like hanging out with you guys. It's good,' he said, and my eyes prickled again. 'So I don't mind that we're heading into an absolute catastrophe of a situation and that we're probably going to get frozen or spend the rest of our lives jumping up and down in temporary classroom 3. I just wanted you guys to know that.' And he looked at the ground, a bit embarrassed.

The Floomins chose that moment to dance again – who knows why, but it was good because it gave us all something to talk about instead of just having an awkward silence after whatever the heck *that* was from G-Dog.

'OK, we've each got a remote control, you three have Frozzypoppers, and you guys have got . . . you've got *moves*.' I gave the Floomins a thumbs-up, not really knowing if they'd understand. They each lifted a stubby little arm back at me, but for all I knew they were saying, 'You are crazy and we're doomed.'

'I'm having an ice cream after this,' I said. 'Who's with me?'

'Yeah!'

'What flavour will you have?' I asked, temporarily distracted and genuinely interested because I had no idea which flav—

'Leeza, we don't have time for this,' said Ishy.

'Right. Yes, of course. OK. Let's go waste some time,' I said. And we marched across the playground to our almost certain defeat.

Chapter 27

ARMY OF ME

The front doors to the school were open. Normally the entrance would look welcoming, but right now it looked like a trap.

I didn't really trust this school any more.

We stood there, in front of the entrance, listening. Well, I was listening, and I think Lemontop was too. The Floomins were swaying slowly from side to side – don't ask me why. Because they wanted to, I suppose. Ishy had chosen this moment to start blowing saliva bubbles, and G-Dog was excavating his nose. Again, because that's what they wanted to do.

We were hardly the Avengers, I thought to myself. I don't know what we were. Or rather, I did. We were us. We weren't heroes. We were very much being ourselves, for better or worse.

Probably worse, I thought, as G-Dog wiped his finger on the side of his tracksuit leg.

'It's very quiet. What do you think is going on?' I said to Lemontop.

'Only the biggest saliva bubble you ever saw!' said Ishy. 'Oh, it burst.'

'Well done, Ishy,' I said, then to Lemontop, 'Where is everyone?'

'Only one way to find out, I suppose,' he said. 'Boys, lock and load. Cover me, I'm going in to scout the area. Hopefully I'll find Captain Chill and Fudge Sundae and I can stop them freezing any more kids.'

I guessed that 'lock and load' was more gun-jargon because Ishy and G-Dog perked right up and each pulled a little lever on their Frozzypoppers that made a ker-chuk sound, which made them nod their heads in appreciation.

'Did I just see you wipe snot on the side of the Frozzypopper?' said Lemontop.

'No,' said G-Dog.

'Good,' said Lemontop, and he ran into the building.

'I totally wiped snot on my Frozzypopper,' said G-Dog.

'You're a beast,' said Ishy.

'G-DOG IS A BEAST!' agreed G-Dog unnecessarily.

I stepped back and craned my neck upwards. The ugly, rusty green spaceship was still parked on the roof, purple gas hissing intermittently from various vents, pipes and nozzles.

'We need to get up there,' I said. 'There's a crawl space above the ceiling you can get to from the stationery cupboard. I think I saw a way to the roof from there so maybe that's where we should go when Lemontop gets— WAIT, NOT YET!'

The Floomins were scampering merrily up the side of the school, heading in a bouncy green tide towards the roof.

I did *not* want them to do that! Almost without thinking I aimed my remote control at them – if they wouldn't listen to me, I could *make* them listen.

'What are you waiting for?' said G-Dog. 'Zap some sense into them! Hey, whoa, don't you point that thing at me!'

I lowered the remote. Because he was wrong and so was I. What was the point of giving them freedom if you took it away the minute they did something you didn't want them to?

The last of them disappeared over the guttering with a skittery pitter-patter.

'They probably have a plan,' I said.

'They also probably know how to fly that ship,' said Ishy. 'Being aliens and everything.'

'Yeah, true, so maybe all we need to do is find an Oooki-Floom and the little ones will hoist it with . . . Oh dear. Not yet, Floomins!' I cried.

With a deep, bassy rumble and a high-pitched whine the ugly green spaceship slowly rose from the roof in a billowing haze of purple emissions. Dangling from two thick metallic cables, a pair of canisters marked 'Happinish' swung like pendulums beneath it.

'Haha, look, the spaceship is shrinking,' laughed G-Dog. 'Who knew they could do that?'

'It's not shrinking,' said Ishy. 'It's getting further away. Uh, Leeza, I think our army of aliens is leaving.'

And Ishy was right, the spaceship was slowly rising higher and higher until . . .

FWOOOOOOOOOOOOOOOM

It shot off like a rocket, up and up and up, trailing a plume of purple exhaust, higher and higher and . . .

Gone.

'Well,' said Ishy.

'Yeah,' I said. 'Up. It's the only way out of here with the force field.'

'Huh,' said Ishy. 'The only way really *is* up.'

'Told you you should've zapped them,' said G-Dog.

'No,' I said. 'If they don't want to help, I'm not going to make them.'

'But they've gone and they've taken the spaceship with them! Your plan was impossible five minutes ago, now it's even impossible-er. No spaceship, no hoisting an alien up, no plan. This is going even worse than I thought it was going to go, and I thought it was going to be a catastrophe.'

'OK, OK. Look, it's disappointing, really disappointing, but . . .'

But what? Was it wrong that in that moment I wished I had a spaceship that I could go *up* in? Just for one little moment. Until the next moment, when I remembered that my parents, and friends, and teachers, and everyone in Owt were either going to be doing what the aliens told them to do, for ever, or they were going to get frozen.

'But look . . . The only way is *not* up,' I said.

'We can go in any direction we choose! The Floomins chose to go up – fine. That was their decision and they probably had their reasons. So we can stay here, feeling sad. We can go in there, feeling scared. We can go home and feel useless. None of the choices are ideal. But you know what? I'm going in. Who's with me?'

'YES! Let's go in!' said Ishy with some urgency. 'Like, right now would be good, I think.'

'Yes, quick! In, in in,' said G-Dog.

Wow. I felt a surge of something. Fear, yes – a bit. But also excitement, and pride, and a warm glow at the fact that my friends were brave enough to . . .

'YOOOOOOOOOOOM,' came the unmistakable booming voice of a big jelly.

Ah, I thought. We're not running *in*, we're running *away*. OK. At least we're moving.

Ah. No. Because . . .

'YOOOOOOOOOOOOOM!'

Another booming bellow from in front of us, inside the school, and another Oooki-Floom oozed through reception towards us, then squeezed itself through the front doors like a bubble from a bubble-blower.

'Oh, poop,' said Ishy. 'That's that, then.'

'YOOOOOOOOM HAVE BEEN SUMMONED TO MEET THE MANAGER OF THE ACADEMY,' it boomed.

Manager, I thought. *Like it's a shop, or a factory. And if it is a shop, what is it selling? And if it's a factory, what is it making? I remember when we used to have a head teacher. That's progress, I suppose!*

And then another voice:

'Up up up, we're reaching for the sky,' it sang, with a broad Owt twang to the accent.

This must be the manager, I thought, and I turned to see.

Ah.

'Ey up, Leeza,' said Mr Gofforth, the pasty man of Owt. 'How's yer belly for spots?'

Chapter 28

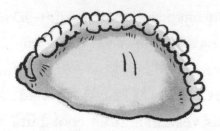

WE JUST WON'T BE DEFEATED

'Yes, I'm the manager,' said Mr Gofforth. 'This is my academy and I think you should know I have the whole town behind me.'

I gasped, because *he was the manager? What?!* And also because he wasn't kidding.

Behind him he had three hundred yellow-clad children, parked, and behind *them*, well, yes, it looked like the whole of Owt, all in yellow tracksuits, a sea of yellow covering the whole of the field surrounding the school.

All motionless. All staring. All smiling. I scanned the crowd hoping, or maybe not hoping, to see my parents. Only two days ago they would have stood out easily – Dad would probably have been wearing a hat that he thought was cool and Mum would have been wearing an expression that suggested she knew the hat was very much not cool. But I couldn't see them. They were just a pair of smiling faces somewhere in the crowd. They were just like everybody else in Owt. I hated that.

As the two monstrous Oooki-Flooms wobbled over to flank Mr Gofforth, Ishy leaned in to me with a confused look on his face.

'Leeza, correct me if I'm wrong but . . . the big baddie is the pasty man? Like, he's the manager? Have I got that right?' said Ishy. 'Wow. Are we supposed to shoot him now or what?'

I was about to say 'no' but I didn't need to. The Oooki-Flooms each shot a gooey tentacle out at lightning speed, snatching Ishy and G-Dog's Frozzypoppers with a Fwap! Fwap!

'Aw, man!' said Ishy. 'We are the absolute worst.'

'G-DOG HAS BEEN DEFROZZLED!' shouted G-Dog unnecessarily.

It was bad. It was really bad, in terms of making my impossible plan even more impossible-er. But on the other hand . . .

'You know what, those guns never suited you. Neither of you,' I said with a sad shrug. 'They just weren't . . . you.'

'Aaaany road up, now I've got your attention, I do think I need to correct you on what you said just now,' said Mr Gofforth. 'I am not a baddie.'

'Well, that's a relief,' I said. Of course, we'd just assumed Mr Gofforth was a baddie because . . .

'You're the baddies, you three idiots,' he said.

'What?' I said. 'What? We're the baddies? We're just—'

'Oh, you're "just", are you? I'll tell you what you're *just*, shall I?' shouted Mr Gofforth, spittle flying from his mouth. 'You're *just* trying to make people unhappy, that's what you're *just*. Look at 'em,' he said, and he gestured at the townsfolk behind him. 'Do they look stressed?

Worried? Tense? Sad? Confused? No. They look happy. And there's a reason for that . . .'

'You've put something in their heads!' I said. 'That's why they're happy!'

'No, no, no,' said Mr Gofforth. 'I mean, yes, technically, I suppose, but also no. They're happy because they are useful. They are serving a purpose. The young 'uns, have you ever seen such a contented bunch in all your days? Why, it reminds me of when I was a nipper . . . paper round, delivering milk, running errands, washing cars, bob-a-jobbing, saving for a mortgage . . . using my time constructively. I smiled like that, you bet I did.'

'But you *chose* to do that. Not everybody wants—'

'Everybody wants to be useful! Your mum and dad, Leeza, and the rest of Owt. Have you ever seen them stand so tall? So proud? They have purpose. They have dignity.' And he beamed proudly. He really was proud of what he had done, of what he was doing. 'I'm doing this for them,' he said.

'But all everyone is doing is jumping up and down and running round in circles!'

'They're smiling. I'm smiling. You guys are smiling, I assume,' he said to the Oooki-Floom on his left.

'I AM SATISFIED WITH CURRENT LEVELS OF OUTPOOOT,' it boomed.

'Champion,' beamed Mr Gofforth. 'He's happy. Everybody's happy, Leeza. Why does that bother you so much, Leeza? Are *you* happy, Leeza?'

I didn't know what to say to that. Was I happy? Sometimes. Sometimes not. Like, take this situation, facing certain defeat at the hands of a mad baker and massive, gooey aliens and countless brainwashed—

'Hang on, hang on. What's *he* doing?' said Mr Gofforth.

'Bum-chikka-bish-chikka-bum-chikka-bish,' said G-Dog, oblivious. He'd clearly lost interest in the whole thing once his gun was taken off him. Classic G-Dog.

'He's beatboxing,' I said with a shrug. 'What do you want me to do about it?'

'I want you to stop him!'

'I can't stop him; he does what he wants.'

'It's just a bit distracting,' whined Mr Gofforth. 'I'm trying to get you to understand why I invited FloomCorp to Owt and he's making it very difficult.'

Meanwhile, I was being distracted by something in the sky, like sunshine glinting off . . . I looked up and then immediately looked back down again. It was a spaceship, slowly and quietly descending. But was this our Floomins or just another FloomCorp truck? Oh, I hoped . . .

'So you say you invited FloomCorp. How did that work?' I asked, desperate to keep him talking.

'What?' said Mr Gofforth, still a bit flustered by G-Dog's activities.

'Can anyone invite an alien invasion?' I said.

'It's not an invasion! It's business. It's just business. There was an advert tucked away in a weird little corner of the Internet. It said something about making oodles of cash, and all you had to do was—'

'Offer to enslave a whole town, that kind of thing?' I said. I kept flicking my eyes up at the sky. The spaceship was getting closer. Come on, Floomins!

'Enslave? You ever see slaves as happy as this? I've improved the town! And it's better than they deserve! Ask yourself this. Did any of them – any of them at all – buy one of my pasties yesterday? Or last week? Or last year? They did not. So here we are. *I've* found another way to make money and *they* are eternally happy and . . . What are *you* doing?'

'Who, me?' said Ishy. 'I'm burping the alphabet. I got to H and now I have to start again.'

Mr Gofforth had asked if I was happy. Right now, weirdly, I couldn't be more happy to be surrounded by my friends, annoying the big baddie.

'You see? This is what I'm talking about. The

three of you! A complete waste of time and energy,' scoffed Mr Gofforth.

'That's me,' said Ishy. 'I was bored. Were you saying anything good? Was he saying anything good, Leeza?'

I smiled. We may not be the Avengers, I thought, but we have our own way of dealing with big baddies. We ignore them. We infuriate them. We do the very things they don't want us to do.

We keep it real. We stay true to ourselves.

I replayed Dad's advice from just two days ago in my mind: *just be yourself.* I replayed it from the point just after his massive fart, because I felt that including the fart would have spoiled the effect. But then I replayed the fart too. And I smiled. I missed Dad's farts. I replayed it again. It really was disgraceful, and funny.

I smiled wider. I couldn't help it. And I think I might have put my hands on my hips, and stood a little taller, and possibly I adjusted my stance slightly. I may even have imagined a cape flapping majestically in the wind behind me.

So this is what it feels like to be a hero, I thought, and then I thought *oh no* because I could feel a familiar tickling in my nose.

'I'll tell you this. In a moment I'm going to stuff little Floomins so far into your heads you won't *believe* how happy you are,' said Mr Gofforth. 'But first I'm going to—'

I never heard what he was going to do first because . . .

AAAAAATCHOOOOO

I sneezed and . . .

KLAKANG!

I looked up and . . .

SWEEEEEEEEEEE

The two canisters dangling from the bottom of the spaceship had come loose and were whistling towards us and . . .

SWOOOOOOOZOOOOM

The spaceship zoomed back into the sky and . . .

Toot

Ishy farted . . .

And . . .

AAAAAATCHO
AAAATCHOO
ATCHOOOOOO

I sneezed helplessly again and again and again and . . .

'Oh, I've had enough of this. Get them!' said Mr Gofforth.

Everything was going horribly, terribly wrong.

Energy Fart

(Noun.) **Phenomenon** that occurs after ingesting an unusually large amount of **energy drinks**

(Actual real definition from a real website of a real thing that really happens on Earth)

Chapter 29

PUMPING ON YOUR STEREO

Plan A had failed, utterly. And we didn't have a Plan B. Whoops.

'Get them, I said!' snarled Mr Gofforth, jabbing a finger towards us, all pretence of joviality gone. I felt for him, I really did, because we really were quite annoying.

SWEEEEEEEE!

The canisters tumbled, but neither Gofforth nor the Oooki-Flooms seemed to have noticed.

The two Oooki-Flooms had pushed out their gelatinous tubes, ready to start pumping Floomins at us. They would only need to hit each of us once and we would be happy for ever.

That was the last thing I wanted. Because right now I was not happy. I was sad, and scared and furious. If I was happy with this situation then why would I want to change it? I wouldn't. And that

would

not

do.

So I pulled my remote control out of my pocket. Here we go, I thought, as G-Dog and Ishy did the same. There was no way we'd be able to hit them all. It was a last stand as pointless as it was ridiculous but, again, I thought pointless and ridiculous suited us quite well.

S w e e e e e e e e e - S P L O O O O M P H - SPLOOOOOMPH

The two canisters landed on, or rather in, the Oooki-Flooms, causing their jellied masses to wipple and ripple. You could see the canisters sinking slowly into their bodies, like someone pushing a Bubblejooce can into a big lime jelly and spoiling somebody's birthday party.

And, like a can of Bubblejooce, the canisters seemed to be emitting bubbles.

'The canisters are leaking,' I said. 'I wonder if that's deliberate.'

Maybe there was a plan after all.

'OOOOOOOOOF!' bellowed one Oooki-Floom.

'BOOOOOBLES!' bellowed the ooother, I mean other.

'Are you getting them or not?' shouted Mr Goftorth.

PLOOP PLOOP PLOOP

Floomins started shooting out of the Oooki-Floom's chutes much faster than before. Whatever was in those canisters was having a propulsive effect. Their chutes were whipping and snaking wildly, throwing their aim off completely.

PLOOPLOOPLOOPLOOPLOOPLOOPLOOP

A cascade of little Floomins was shooting

out of the Oookis like jammy machine-gun bullets. They bounced off walls, splooched on windows, boinged across the tarmac of the playground.

PLOOPLOOPLOOPLOOPLOOPLOOPLOOP

I tried clicking my remote at them as they flew but there were so many of them! Thankfully they were hitting everything so hard they seemed dazed.

Ishy sniffed the air quizzically as he clicked. I did the same – there was definitely a familiar tang in the air but I couldn't put my finger on it.

The PLOOPING stopped abruptly to be replaced by something that sounded like . . . well, I mean, it rather sounded like . . .

'They're farting,' said G-Dog, delighted.

And they really were. Loudly and continuously. The one on the left was making a high-pitched squeaky kind of noise, like air escaping from the neck of a balloon, while the one on the right was more of a bassy, wet duvet-lifter.

'**OOOOOOOOOOOOO, THIS IS HOOOORRIBLE,**' boomed lefty Oooki-Floom.

'**IT WOOOON'T STOOOOOOP!**' boomed righty.

'Oh, for pity's sake,' tutted Mr Gofforth. 'Get a grip! It's just side effects. Better out than in, after all.'

Ishy sniffed the air once more. 'That smell, it's ... Oh man, haha, it smells just like Bubblejooce,' he laughed. 'Weird coincidence! I think the big jellies are energy-farting.'

It was strange – whatever FloomCorp was making here, this Happinish, it was obviously not very good for them at all.

'G-Dog,' I shouted. 'You heard the man. *Better out than in*. Which means *in* is worse. Which means ...'

But I didn't have to tell him what to do. It just came naturally to him.

'G-DOG GOTS TWO OF YOUR FIVE A DAY!' shouted G-Dog a little unnecessarily, and he barrelled towards the Oooki-Flooms. Somehow he already had a banana in each hand. Where *was* he getting them from?

'Ishy, channel-hop,' I said.

But Ishy was way ahead of me, aiming his remote and clicking clicking clicking, and I was doing the same.

We were just doing what we normally do when school is out.

CLICK CLICK CLICK CLICK

FLOOOOOTCH! FLOOOOOTCH!

G-Dog stoppered the beleaguered, bubbling Oooki-Flooms with two expertly rammed bananas.

'OOOO, WHAT NOOOOW?' boomed lefty.

'I'M GROOOOOOOWING!' boomed righty.

And they were right, they did seem to be expanding slightly.

'G-DOG DOIN' WHAT HE DO!' shouted G-Dog, and I was starting to feel like the shouting *was* necessary, somehow. It wouldn't be G-Dog without the shouting.

Me and Ishy were clicking our remotes like we were hunting for the exact right anime to binge on the streamers. As we hit them the dazed, newly plooped Floomins started twitching, then rocking, then full-on dancing.

'What are you doing to my drivers?!' said Mr Gofforth. 'Stop it right now! You're making them useless!'

It was quite the scene. The Floomins were whirling, hot-stepping, dabbing and doing the twist all over the place. The Oooki-Flooms were slowly expanding. Mr Gofforth was shaking with fury but powerless to do anything about any of it.

I just could not stop smiling. I was having a blast, honestly. I almost forgot we were here to foil an alien invasion, the whole thing was so much fun.

Then my eyes scanned the scene and my smile faltered. They say smiles are infectious, but I looked out across the playground and beyond at the sea of yellow-clad friends, family, teachers and townsfolk, each one infected by a smile that did not belong on their face, and my own smile faltered and I remembered why we were here.

We were here to save the town.

We just needed to freeze the aliens and we'd be away. Unfortunately the Frozzypoppers were still very much in the grasp of the ever-inflating Oooki-Flooms.

My plan had come unstuck once more. What now? I wondered if anyone might have a suggestion. Something caught my eye – a single Floomin waving its stubby little arms by my foot. It tugged my trouser leg. What did it want?

Was it Pickle? They all looked the same but I had a feeling – the strangest feeling.

P-TOOF! P-TOOF!

Oh heck. The bananas were ejected from the Oooki-Flooms, which was bad news. Then each

Oooki shot out a gummy attacktacle and Ishy and G-Dog were suddenly pinned by their necks to the wall of the school.

'Let them go!' I shouted as my boys struggled, legs kicking, to be free of the tentacles. 'Please, Mr Gofforth, tell them to let them go!'

Pickle was still tugging at my trouser leg.

'Not now,' I hissed, with a flick of my foot.

'No, no, I don't think I will,' said Mr Gofforth. 'Sorry, chuck, but you three are the only thing stopping this factory from being a success.'

'Please, Mr Gofforth, please. You have a choice here. Please, you can stop this.'

'I'll be honest, Leeza, I'm not sure I can,' he shrugged. 'I mean, it's pretty much done now. What, am I going to release everyone, say sorry and then we'll all let bygones be bygones? No, I think I need to see this through.'

Pickle was back tugging at my leg.

'What do you WANT?' I said, irritated, and I looked down and Pickle looked up at me and I *knew*. Somehow I knew what Pickle wanted.

Pickle wanted to help me.

It was a big decision. I didn't think twice. My friends were being hurt.

'Yes,' I said. 'Yes, do it.'

And Pickle leapt towards my face.

Chapter 30

WOW

Oh boy. Oh wow. Oh wowow oh boy oh boy.

What was going on?

I felt AMAZING. I felt mad energy coursing through my body. I felt better than I had ever felt before.

What was going on?

I think I had a Pickle in my head.

YOOOM ARE UPGRADED. YOOOM CAN HELP YOOOR FRIENDS. YOOOM ARR LEEZA AND PICK-OOOL.

It was not so much a voice in my head, more just something that I suddenly *knew*.

Pickle's thoughts and my thoughts were sort of the same.

Why are we doing this? we asked.

FOR THANK YOOOM, we answered.

'Excellent, excellent. One down, two to go,' I could hear Mr Gofforth chuntering smugly.

He thought I had any old Floomin in my head. He had no idea it was my Pickle. He had no idea what was going to happen next!

Thing is, neither did I.

I felt very ... very. So very very. More very than I had ever felt before.

I jumped. Wow, did I ever jump! I twirled in the air, three times. I landed. I laughed. I cartwheeled over to Mr Gofforth. I had never cartwheeled before. I was right next to him. My gosh, it felt like I could do anything.

'Remember,' I said. 'Remember I gave you a choice.'

'What?' he spluttered. 'Get over there with the rest of them. Get ready for school.' And I laughed at him because the idea of anyone telling me what to do was laughable right now. I was making all my own choices.

'School's out,' I said. 'Wait here. I'll be back.'

I leapt over to the Oooki-Flooms and yanked each of their attacktacles in turn, freeing poor Ishy and G-Dog, who dropped, coughing and gasping for breath.

'YOOOOOOM ARE DISRUPTING OOOR PLANS,' boomed lefty Oooki a little unnecessarily. Of course I was.

'Of course I am,' I said. 'Gimme that.' I snatched a Frozzypopper off lefty Oooki and

FRAKL

I froze righty Oooki.

'YOOOM WILL STOOOP THIS!'

Lefty shot an attacktacle towards me but I dodged it easily, leapt ten metres into the air and . . .

FRAKL

I never heard any more from lefty Oooki.

YOOOM ARR STRONG BUT YOOOM ARR NOT HAPPY YET, we thought as we made a perfect landing. **PICK-OOOL CAN MAKE YOOOM HAPPY.**

No, we thought. *I can make myself happy. I just need to help my friends, and family, and everyone else, then I'll be smiling, don't you worry. We just need to hoist these alien lollies into the air and . . .*

PICK-OOOL FRENNNDS CAN HELP YOOOR FRENNNDS FOR THANK YOOOM.

And don't ask me how, but I knew Pickle was sending a message, asking for help from all the other Floomins, the ones in the spaceship.

And as I cartwheeled to my dazed and confused boys, my Ishy and G-Dog, and picked them up and dusted them down, the ugly green spaceship had descended and was hoisting the two frozen Oooki-Flooms into the air on the end of two snakey silver cables.

'Are you two OK?' I said.

'G-DOG HAS FELT BETTER BUT IS HAPPY TO SEE YOU!' shouted G-Dog.

Click-POOOOSh. glug glug glug. Ishy gave a thumbs-up as he downed a Bubblejooce, then

250

he belched the word 'fine' and I knew they were both OK.

'What about you, Leeza? Are you OK?' said G-Dog.

'Yeah, what happened? How did the big dudes get frozen? When did they get hoisted up there?' said Ishy.

They must have missed what I'd been up to, on account of being pinned to the wall of the school. I didn't really know how to explain what had happened so for the moment I didn't.

'Oh, you know,' I said, vaguely waving my hands. 'Anyway, you both ready for a disco light show?' I asked with a smile.

'G-DOG LOCK AND LOAD!'

Burp!

We were ready.

Toot!

OK, now we were definitely ready. Thanks, Ishy.

We aimed our remotes at the dangling alien mirrorballs and we clicked.

And clicked. And clicked.

And our little remote controls fired invisible light at the frozen Oooki-Flooms and . . .

It was beautiful.

The whole playground was bathed in a delirious and ever-shifting light show. The light danced across our faces, and over the faces of all our families and friends and their friends and families. A laser light show the size of a town, like every school disco and wedding dance floor and New Year firework display rolled into one. And with a sound like popcorn popping times a million, six thousand Floomins plopped out of six thousand nostrils.

'Stop it. Stop it, stop it, stop it!' shrieked Mr Gofforth. But there was no stopping it. He looked very pretty under the lights and I wondered if he realised that and whether it might change his mood if I told him. Probably not.

The Floomins fell to the ground like autumn in bogeyland and they danced. They danced and danced, and there was something so joyful and inclusive about their moves that the newly liberated ex-Driven, the children, the grown-ups and the teachers, were driven to dance too, dazed as they were. A town's worth of humans dancing with aliens, mad moves never seen before on any dance floor on this planet.

'WHAT IS THE MEANING OF ALL THIS POINTLESS MOOOVEMENT?' boomed an Oooki-Floom.

'IT IS UNPRODOOOCTIVE! STOOOP THIS AT ONCE!'

Amidst all this happiness we hadn't noticed two more Oooki-Flooms wooobling towards us.

'Freeze 'em!' yelled Ishy, but I shook my head.

'Keep clicking,' I said. 'I'll deal with them.'

YOOOM COULD KICK THEM INTO SPACE, we thought.

Could we? we thought, and the idea made me excited and frightened all at once.

YOOOM COULD MAKE THEM LEAVE.

But no. No. Kicking and punching, even the cartwheeling – it wasn't me. *I think I can*

253

convince them to go, we thought. *Please, take some time off. Have a dance.*

I WILL STAY JUST IN CASE.

I marched over to the Oooki-Flooms.

'THIS NOOONSENSE IS BAD FOR PRODOOOCTION,' said one.

'It's producing happiness,' I said. 'Actual happiness, not whatever Happinish is. You don't dance like that if you're sad. It's also producing some killer moves. Look at that.'

I gestured over to where I could see Mrs Ramshaw attempting a caterpillar next to Miss Duffield, who looked happy and relaxed as she jumped from foot to foot, windmilling her arms like a loon.

'WE OFFERED YOOOM HAPPINESS,' said the Oooki-Floom. **'AND THIS IS HOW YOOOM THANK US.'**

'Thanks,' I said. 'But we have our own ways of producing happiness. You dancing?' I offered a hand.

'WE MUST LEAVE THIS PLACE,'

said the Oooki-Floom. **'IT IS NO GOOOD FOR BUSINESS.'**

'You should try selling quality pasties here,' said Mr Gofforth, who had sidled over from wherever he'd been hiding. 'It's a heckin' nightmare. Listen, if you're leaving, would you mind taking me? I mean, look at this,' he said, gesturing around at everyone dancing. 'What a colossal waste of time. Honestly, I'm on the wrong planet.'

But the Oooki-Floom ignored him. **'WE APOOOLOGISE FOR ANY INCONVENIENCE,'** it boomed. **'THIS FACILITY IS CLOOOSED. ON A PERSONAL LEVEL, MAY I WISH YOU EVERY UNHAPPINESS GOING FORWARD. I HOPE NEVER TO VISIT THIS STOOOPID PLANET AGAIN. YOU ARE, INDEED, A HECKING NIGHTMARE.'**

We'd won.

Maybe it was the light show, maybe it was being in the middle of the greatest dance party ever, but I was so happy and relaxed I was about to make some sort of speech, about happiness being a gift you give yourself, which can't be bought, or sold, or forced on you, and some other stuff, maybe something about ice cream? But thankfully I never got a chance because the Oooki-Floom was suddenly engulfed in a searing column of the brightest white light, and then the light and the Oooki were gone. Across the way another dazzling spotlight whisked the other Oooki-Floom away, and from my vantage point in the playground I saw columns of light appear and disappear across Owt, until there were only two big Oookis left, the frozen ones dangling from the spaceship.

'Don't go!' wailed Mr Gofforth. 'Take me with you! Please! Take me with you!'

The frozen Oooki-Flooms said nothing. And then a flash of white and they too had disappeared.

Mr Gofforth sank to his knees and sobbed. 'I hate it here,' he sniffled. 'You people do my head in.'

I felt sorry for him, even though all this was his fault. He'd tried to make himself feel better by changing the way everyone around him felt, instead of by changing himself. It's an easy mistake to make.

YOOOM CAN MAKE HIM HAPPY, we thought. **STICK ONE OF MY FRENNNDS UP HIS NOOOSTRIL.**

No, we thought. *Let him find his own way. He needs happiness, not Happinish. I think we all do, really.*

I patted Mr Gofforth on the back. I didn't know what else to do. I looked out at the scene that was causing him so much anguish.

The light show had gone with the Oooki-Flooms but the dancing had continued. Smiling faces, groovy moves, aliens and humans spurring each other on like an intergalactic dance-off where everyone was a winner. Everything had turned out OK . . .

'RUN!' came an anguished shout from within the school. 'Run! There's a monster in here!' And the ice-cream men burst from the school entrance in a massive hurry.

Chapter 31

GROOVE IS IN THE HEART

'Whoa,' said Captain Chill. 'Wait a minute.'

The three ice-cream men stopped running and started gawping.

'Hi,' I said. 'Everything OK?'

'I am not a monster, I am a pupil and I demand to be taught some history!' shouted the scary monster from inside the school.

Charlotte Actually leapt out of the entrance doors, did two somersaults and executed a perfect Marvel superhero crouch-landing.

She looked around.

'Whoa,' she said.

'Whoa exactly. What's happened here?' said Captain Chill.

'Well, I'll tell you what happened,' said Ishy. 'Leeza here—'

'It all just sorted itself out while you and Charlotte were fighting in the school,' I said hurriedly. 'The Oooki-Flooms just sort of gave up and left.'

'Did they?' said Captain Chill.

'Yes,' I said. 'Unless maybe it was the massive, time-consuming battle between you and Charlotte in the school over how exactly to deal with the aliens that scared them off. That might be what happened.'

'Do you think?' said Captain Chill with a hopeful smile.

'Do you?' I said, and I left him to figure that one out.

'Guys, this is . . . this is awesome news,' said Lemontop. 'I . . . I am so . . . I am so huh-huh-

260

happy right now-how-how-hoo.' He was ugly-crying so hard he could hardly get his words out. He was a man in perfect tune with his own emotions.

'I'm going to get ice creams for everyone,' said Fudge Sundae. 'What do you all want?'

'Three scoops, one each of chocolate, lime and vanilla, please,' I said without thinking.

'None for me or Miss Duffield,' said Charlotte. She was leading poor Miss Duffield by the hand towards the school. 'We'll have some after history.'

Miss Duffield's face was twitching and her eyes were red around the rims. She was back to her old, nervous, anxious self. *You're welcome*, I thought.

I went and gathered my boys for a group hug.

'L-DOG'S PLAN WAS LIT!' shouted G-Dog.

L-Dog. It was a change from Leeza Sneezer, I supposed.

'But none of it was really my plan at all,' I said.

'Yeah, but your plan got us where we needed to be. None of this would have happened if you hadn't done what you did. So well done, Leeza!' said Ishy. 'Not gonna lie, I had a feeling your plan would be a waste of time but I had no idea it would be the greatest waste of time I've ever been a part of. Well done! You dancing?'

'Definitely,' I said. 'Definitely.'

'We just wanted to say thank you for distracting the Floomins while we foiled the alien invasion,' said Captain Chill, who had marched back over with quite the skip in his step.

'You *what*!?' said Ishy, his tone full of outrage.

I nudged him and said, 'It was nothing, no problem. One thing is bugging me though,' I added. 'This place was a factory, right? They were making something called Happinish, but does anyone know what that actually is?'

'No idea!' said the Captain with a grin. 'Doesn't matter! They don't make it here any more. Hey, how about an ice cream AND a can of Bubblejooce for everyone?'

'Ooooooh, Bubblejooce!' said Ishy. 'Don't mind if I do!'

'And after that we'd like a word,' said the Captain, giving me a cheery wink. 'We might have a job for you.'

'So, about that dance,' said Ishy.

'Yes,' I said. 'But first I want to find my mum and dad.'

Now he was freed from eternal happiness Dad would once again be the absolute worst dancer. Totally embarrassing. A flat-footed, enthusiastically windmilling catastrophe. And Mum would be there with him, carefully stepping from one foot to the other, arms moving slightly off the beat, the most sensible, self-conscious, wonderful mum-dancing you ever saw. I really, really wanted to dance with them.

But first, I thought, I needed to quickly catch up with Fudge Sundae to maybe change my ice-cream order. *Lime?* What was I thinking?

IMPORTANT MEMO

Earth is now out of bounds. REPEAT we are closing all factories on that stooopid planet. It's too much hassle. We'll open factories on other, less annoying planets, and leave Earth to the other two alien energy drink manufacturers and those crazy tentacle-heads that make spray-on cheese.

(Internal FloomCorp ooomail)

EPILOOOG

ALRIGHT

Mr Gofforth sold his shop and moved out of town shortly afterwards. Owt is a small place and rumours spread fast, and once it got round that he'd invited alien invaders into town, who had enslaved the whole population for a couple of days – well, you can imagine how embarrassed he must have felt.

He never apologised though, not that I heard.

The next day's newspaper carried the headline 'LOCAL GIRL FOILS ATTEMPT'.

It was quite a vague story. The school had been overrun by something-or-other, and a possible chemical leak had affected the rest of the town, but it was quite clear who had saved the day. The photo showed a beaming Charlotte Actually, who was quoted as saying, 'I don't know if I'd call myself a hero, but this will certainly look good on my CV!' I didn't mind. It suited her more than it suited me.

My parents ditched the yellow tracksuits immediately and went back to being my unfit, argumentative, pain-in-the-neck mum and dad. Dad in particular really ramped up the awful, terrible, dreadful jokes and I can't tell you how happy that has made me. And I can't say I actually stand and applaud when he farts at inappropriate moments, but I don't kick up a fuss either. Dad's gonna Dad.

Occasionally, when walking round Owt, I'll see people being grumpy, or disappointed, or jealous, or argumentative and I think *I did that*, and I feel . . . Well, I have mixed emotions, but that's what being a human is all about, isn't it?

Ishy is still Ishy. He went through a bad patch when he realised he had never said, 'These aliens are really getting up my nose,' at any point during the invasion but he soon cheered up. He and G-Dog have formed a street dance troupe called Floomin Moovin, which is . . . Well, once seen, never forgotten.

Speaking of the Floomins, they all flew off in the FloomCorp truck. I say 'all'; nobody ever thought to count how many there had been. Some might have chosen to stick around, who knows?

We, sorry, *I* am still allergic to most things. A friend offered to cure my allergies, as a kind of upgrade, if you like, but after some thought I decided that sneezing at exactly the wrong time was my thing, so I politely declined and my friend respected my wishes. Then, however, he offered to stick around and help me jump a little higher and run a little faster occasionally, and really, isn't that what friends do anyway, so who could say no to an offer like that? Would you?

I've got a new schnozzdongle. Two, actually. One to stick up my nose and a bigger, more powerful one to fire at aliens, should the need arise. I have a Saturday job as an ice-cream man, so it has come in handy once or twice.

Of course, I had to choose an ice cream name. It took a while but eventually I settled on **[note to my dear publisher, please can I add my ice cream name when I've chosen one? I promise I will think of one before the book is published. thx Leeza x]**.

So whenever you see an ice-cream van trundle by, chiming an eerie, echoey version of the *Blue Peter* theme or 'Greensleeves', don't feel like you have to salute or bang some pots and pans or anything, but maybe just silently thank them for everything they do. They may not get it right every time, but they are our best and only line of defence against alien invaders. Also, they sell ice cream on sunny days and what could be more heroic than that?

But even heroes need help. So please, please keep eating ice cream, as much of it as you possibly can, any flavour you like. It really is your duty, if you want to help the ice-cream men protect us all.

Oooki Flooms

Jelly-like creatures from somewhere near the Ooort Cloud of planetoids. They are known to be dangerous, and big. Really big. If you want to picture how big they are, imagine a jelly as big as a double decker bus. Can you picture that? WOAH, THAT'S TOO BIG! Make it smaller, like the size of a big van, or two small vans stacked on top of each other, or quarter of a fire engine. That's better. Now make that quarter of a fire engine green, and see-through, and wobbly, and give it quite an unpleasant personality and wildly hazardous tentacles and WELL DONE you've imagined exactly what an Oooki Floom looks like.

(From *Know Your Aliens: An Ice Cream Man Primer*)

Floomins

Small, jelly-like aliens known for their ability to 'drive' other species by entering their brains through their nose holes. This process often confers extra strength and agility to the host creatures, while also removing their free will. Floomins are also quite good at dancing, apparently. I say 'good' – they wouldn't win Strictly but they are energetic and enthusiastic, like a five-year-old at a wedding disco.

(From *Know Your Aliens: An Ice Cream Man Primer*)

WE GOT 99 PROBLEMS
BUT A 99 AIN'T ONE.

IT'S MOSTLY ALIENS. WOULD YOU LIKE A 99?

(The Ice Cream Men motto)

ACKNOOOWLEDGEMENTS

I CAN'T TELL YOU HOW MUCH I ENJOY WRITING THESE DAFT STORIES (EVEN WHEN I'M MOPING AROUND PRETENDING I DON'T), SO THANK YOOOM TO EVERYBODY WHO HAS HELPED ME WRITE THEM AND TO EVERYBODY WHO HAS PLAYED THEIR PART IN TURNING THEM INTO BOOKS, AND TO EVERYBODY WHO'S TAKEN THE TIME TO READ THEM. IT MEANS THE WORLD TO ME.

BUT MOST ESPECIALLY, THANK *YOU*. YEAH, **YOU**.

THANK YOU. THANK YOU SO VERY MUCH.

YOU KNOW WHO YOU ARE.

AND YOU SHOULD KNOW YOUR ICE-CREAM NAME IS 'MINT'.

LOOOVE FROM JAMES X

I live near a biscuit factory. Sounds like a dream come true, right?

But it's not all fun and Jammie Dodgers. You see, the biscuit factory is really a Super-Secret Science Lab. Everyone pretends it makes biscuits. It just makes life easier.

Until today. Because the biscuit factory tore a hole between dimensions, and now HUGE ORANGE MONSTERS are climbing through.

Oh, and if we don't do something, the world is going to go

KABLOOEY

in the next thirty minutes.

NOT ON MY WATCH.
You coming?

'So funny you'll snort custard creams out of your nose' MR J DODGER

ABOUT JAMES HARRIS

JAMES HARRIS IS A TALLISH HUMAN FROM MIDDLESBROUGH. HE IS MOST LIKELY NOT A RABBIT IN DISGUISE ALTHOUGH HE DOES ENJOY SALADS AND HIDING SO WE CAN'T BE 100% SURE.

HE HAS ALWAYS LOVED MAKING STUFF WITH HIS FRIENDS: HOME-MADE COMICS, MUSIC, COMEDY SHOWS, ZINES, DAFT LITTLE FILMS, AWESOME SANDWICHES, ALL THAT.

IN 2019, HE WON THE HACHETTE CHILDREN'S NOVEL PRIZE AT THE NORTHERN WRITERS' AWARDS WITH HIS FIRST EVER BOOK *THE UNBELIEVABLE BISCUIT FACTORY.*

NOW HE'S GONE AND WRITTEN ANOTHER ONE. SOMEONE SHOULD PROBABLY STOP HIM BEFORE HE TRIES TO DO IT AGAIN.